Spacef s

A Novel by Gerry A. Saunders

The Martian Factor

My SpaceFed StarShip Series is one continuous story over 10 books.

The thrilling, action-packed Sci-fi space adventure saga begins.

12

Other Books by this Author

SpaceFed StarShips Trilogy.
Book 1. Battles at Zeta Reticuli.
Book 2. Battle for Delta Pavonis.
Book 3. An Alliance at Kepler.

SpaceFed StarShips Series.
Book 4. Death of Time.
Book 5. Acarea. A Triumph or Disaster.
Book 6. The Garoden War. Part 1. Into the Fire.
Book 7. The Garoden War. Part 2. Military Gamble.
Book 8. Galactic War. (Up Time, Down).
Book 9. Battle for Time.

Plus: The Definitive StarShips Trilogy, in one book.
 The Martian Factor (Prequel)

http://www.spacefedbooks.com

About the book

We thought we were alone. Oblivious to the fact that we weren't. We were easy pickings. Unprepared mentally and technically to survive.

The Earth Federation came into being in 2146. By 2235, however, the E.F. had founded the present Space Federation and banned all military operations in Space.

In the spring of 2301, the Space Federation finally started the acceptance trials for its latest interstellar StarShip, Andromeda, built at the Mars Starship construction facility.

Andromeda was the first in a new generation of ships equipped with the latest weaponry and advanced Comms systems. While the upgraded Warp drive made it possible for Andromeda to reach further into deep space than ever before.

Andromeda's first mission was to find the Starship Hawk, which had been commissioned in 2290 and sent to Procyon in Canis Major. But had disappeared under mysterious circumstances and was feared lost.

Afterward, Andromeda would attempt to locate the nuclear-pulse-powered settler Starship, Acarea, launched almost two hundred years earlier.

However, things don't start well. A Space transport ship piloted by Captain Frank Richardson en route to Mar's Docks experiences alien interference.

Then a violent clash with Earth's banned Space Navy, who attempt to take over Andromeda during her acceptance trials, leaves humanity's first real starship in danger.

.

This Prequel starts the series off with a bang. And provides an exciting, informative, and action-packed lead into the saga. With tantalizing references to future points as it leads you into Book 1.

Content

Chapter 1

Celebration

Stardate: 2290.65

Captain Michael Turner was feeling apprehensive as he sat in his command chair watching the Mars facility's tugs move the Starship Hawk out to a safe distance from the Mars station. Then Hawk would transfer to her final warp-departure location under her own power. Where her warp field wouldn't affect the Mars Starship manufacturing facility.

Turner was disappointed that he would miss the completion of the Mars Station's fifth construction bay. While other bays already held newer and sleeker-looking starships in the process of being assembled.

During her acceptance trials, Hawk had successfully micro-jumped there and back several times, over the 40 million kilometers needed to reach a clear area between Mars and Earth.

However, during the first two jumps, Turner felt an unexpected hesitation when Hawk created her warp bubble. This had made him feel very uneasy, and, in his opinion, the warp drive wasn't a hundred percent stable.

Nevertheless, Hawk had passed her acceptance targets with flying colors.

Hawk had a total jump capability of thirty-five light-years. And had just been cleared to jump the shorter distance of eleven-point five light-years, directly to Procyon. Which allowed for twenty-three light years each way, plus a safety margin.

Turner glanced at the other two crewmembers on the bridge, Science officer Peter Bracket and his Chief Officer and pilot, Nick Chambers. Both of whom were busy studying the continuous data flow. In particular, data from Astro and Engineering.

"Captain, we are at the Secondary-marker," Bracket stated as confirmation of the Tug's separation from Hawk appeared on his science station display.

Seconds later, Mission Control's welcome voice came over the bridge's sound system.

"Starship Hawk, you are authorized to move to your primary jump location."

"Thank you, control," Turner acknowledged, then nodded approval to Bracket and Chambers.

"Are we clear, Anna?" Turner audibly questioned his A.I. The central A.I. had been named Anna by Hawk's crew.

"Yes. No obstructions in our path. All systems are clear," the AI reported.

"Prep to move," Turner ordered while tapping Engineering's icon. The chief engineer's face instantly appeared on Turner's screen.

"We're ready, captain," Patrick Powers confirmed, anticipating Turner's question. "Sub-light drive power is at thirty-four percent. More than enough to get us to our jump location."

"Only good enough if we generate sufficient power when we exit close to Procyon."

"We will have by then, Captain," Powers confidently stated.

"Okay, we're about to get underway," Turner said, tapping engineering's icon to Off.

Then Turner visualized their six rear-facing, highly polished emitters flaring. Sending a whitish-violet light beam across space. With the beam's focal point some four-hundred meters behind it. This stream of heavy photons produced a pull on a heavy nucleus, giving the drive greater push power.

"Track clear. Authorization required," Anna prompted.

"Go," Turner ordered.

Almost instantly, Turner felt a slight acceleration which slowly increased.

"Beam pressure holding steady," Bracket stated.

"Five minutes to primary jump location," Anna added.

The following five minutes passed in silence. As everyone realized that this was *it*. There was no going back; the jump to greatness, or oblivion, was here and now.

"Hawk. Your warp window will be open for eleven minutes. You are clear to execute jump," came mission control's final instruction.

"Thank you," Turner replied.

"Good luck to you all," mission control added.

"Now we really are on our own," Turner muttered.

"Final checks now," he ordered. As he quickly checked the other 29 crew members' readiness status.

Then brought up the wire mesh representation of the Warp field as it was being generated in real-time.

An incredible amount of energy was needed to pulse the two Jump-rings and fold space long enough for the warp crystal to create the wormhole. All of this had to happen in a precise sequence.

The original idea of generating a warp bubble around a ship and sustaining it while moving through space proved impossible due to the enormous energy required.

"Astro?" Turner called, and Mike Ferguson's face appeared on his secondary screen.

"All locked in, Captain. As ordered, our exit point will be one light-year from Procyon's primary target."

"Good," Turner replied. Then called Engineering, and Mike Ferguson's image morphed into the face of Patrick Powers.

"We're ready, Captain."

"Stay sharp," he said, then nodded at Bracket and Chambers.

"Ready," both acknowledged in unison.

"Right. Status, please, Anna?"

"Systems optimal, Captain."

"Initiate jump sequence…. Now," Turner ordered.

Then he suddenly felt a massive jolt as the warp pulse surged into Hawk's Jump rings. While his real-time wire mesh presentation showed space folding in front of them.

He was almost sure that he saw a hesitation in the warp field creation. But the warp crystal successfully punched a hole in spacetime. Then the wormhole formed, with Hawk seeming to stretch as it plunged into the wormhole.

Turner's surroundings also stretched, and he felt like he'd left part of himself behind. It was almost like he was surging past a catapult's arms under immense power.

For a moment, nothing, and Turner felt as if he was stationary, then he felt nauseous momentarily as if the rest of his body had finally caught up with him.

Turner was relieved. They were now traveling through the wormhole, in transit to Procyon, and in good shape.

Chapter 2

Starship Hawk

Stardate: 2290.7

The Starship, Hawk, had finally set out on her maiden voyage. And was now en route from the Mars station to Procyon, in Canis Major, through the artificially generated wormhole.

Once Hawk arrived in the Procyon system, she would search for the missing nuclear pulse-powered settler Starship, Acarea. Which had been launched two hundred years earlier.

After which, Hawk would explore the Star systems local to Procyon. These were expected to include at least two habitable planets.

Captain Michael Turner felt the Hawk shudder briefly, then everything returned to normal.

But Science officer Peter Bracket looked worried as he studied the Hawk's secondary jump-ring controller data.

"That's very unusual, Captain!" Bracket exclaimed."

Turner left his command chair and quickly joined his science officer on hearing this. Then, Nick Chambers took the hint and linked his display to the image on Bracket's screen.

"What was it?" Turner asked.

"See that spike..., there?" Bracket said, highlighting it for them on the display while using his finger to expand the area.

"H'mm, it looks as if it's an unbalanced controller. If so, it could cause the wormhole to collapse," Chambers muttered.

"Agreed, and that's the danger. Another spike like that, and we would drop out of warp for sure," Bracket agreed.

Then Turner pressed Bracket's engineering tab to query it with Powers.

"We're already looking into it, Captain," came Patrick Powers' immediate response.

"Yes, the problem seems to be in the auto-leveling link between the secondary ring and the forward crystal," science officer Bracket suggested.

"That's where we're concentrating our efforts," Powers added.

"Well, make it quick. We'll monitor your progress from the bridge," Captain Turner replied and closed the contact.

The link was imperative to keep the wormhole open. And Turner knew precisely what an out-of-balance secondary jump ring link to Hawk's nose-crystal would do. The best-case scenario would be possible damage to Hawk's outside sensor grids. Worst case, Hawk would be ripped apart by the collapsing wormhole.

"Spiking!" Bracket yelled out in disbelief as Hawk shuddered.

Then Captain Turner involuntarily cursed as his surroundings rippled and power left the ship. He felt as if he was inside a collapsing rubber balloon with his body jerking, stretching, and twisting as if he was just a doll.

Turner felt the pain of being bounced around the Bridge and wished he was in his own seat, like Bracket and Chambers.

Then came a sudden calm. Causing Hawk's crew to physically throw up from the damaging effects of the forced exit from the collapsing wormhole.

By now, the Hawk was in normal space and powerless. But the effects of their unplanned exit continued to ripple through the ship for a while.

"Bloody hell," Turner exclaimed, attempting to stand up as power slowly returned to the ship.

Science officer Peter Bracket waited with bated breath as Anna, the central AI, rebooted, and his science station came back online.

Then the ship's status, having been re-checked by Hawk's central AI, began to display again.

"Captain, the data is not yet complete," the AI warned.

Then Brackett heard Engineering's Patrick Powers' groggy voice emanating from his console.

"Patrick, are you okay?" he asked.

"Yes. But we only managed to locate the problem just before we crashed out of warp."

"That's great news, Patrick. We couldn't find what the problem was from here. Because the AI was still re-building lost links," Bracket explained.

"We were lucky, Captain. It looks like one of the laser couplers between the ring and nose crystal failed. Once we're fully operational, it'll take about twenty minutes to replace it," Powers reported.

"Okay. As fast as you can," Bracket urged and closed the contact.

"Nick, hyper-link an update to Earth right away."

"On it, Captain. I reckon we're all lucky to be alive," Nick said, sounding more upbeat as Turner returned to his seat.

"Hopefully, we'll stay that way," Turner agreed. Then settled back in his command seat and selected Astro.

"Yes, captain," Astro's Mike Ferguson answered.

"I appreciate your star charts don't have any references from this point in space. But we need a location, and an exit reference point close to Procyon, as soon as possible."

"It might take a while, Captain. We'll have to backtrack to get the star's configuration and distance from our ship to predict Procyon's location on exit."

"I know. Just do what you can," Turner frustratedly replied.

"Will do, Captain. At least the AI is now fully operational. So that should speed up the process."

"Yes. Keep me in the loop, Mike," Turner ordered and closed his contact. He then selected medical, and Jan Taylor answered.

"Any casualties?"

"A few with cuts and bruises, but our scans indicate that all twenty-seven of the ship's complement is fine."

"Thanks, Jan," Turner acknowledged and closed the link. Then he selected 'Broadcast.'

"Listen up, crew, we're probably stuck here for a few hours. So, get some food and rest when you've finished what you're doing… Over and out."

Then Captain Turner relaxed, knowing that his crew was quite capable of getting Hawk ready to jump for Procyon again without him distracting them.

He decided not to go to his cabin. Instead, he stayed on the bridge and ordered a meal from the limited menu that was now showing on his command chair's console.

Moments later, a service droid glided in and delivered his meal.

"Thank you," Turner automatically said, and the Droid quickly turned and left on another mission.

Then Chambers interrupted Turner's thoughts.

"Captain, I've successfully sent a Hyperlink report to Earth, notifying them we'll report again when we arrive at Procyon."

"Perfect."

After eating, Turner tapped the 'Call Droid' icon to collect his empty container. Checked everything was progressing well. Then took a nap.

Captain Turner was woken by a contact alarm sounding throughout the Hawk. His heart was pounding, and he felt sick.

"Turn that alarm off," Captain Turner yelled, more startled by the noise than anything else.

"Well…. What caused that…? Anyone…?"

"A ship has exited warp about forty-one kilometers out," Barret nervously stated as Hawk's sensors tried to scan the newcomer.

Then Turner's heart sank as he looked through the Hawk's forward windows. At first, he couldn't see anything clearly, then he concentrated his gaze and could just about make out what seemed to be a long, cigar-shaped, and copper-colored vessel.

Although it was far away, in his mind, it appeared to be more menacing than he could ever have imagined.

"As far as we can make out, Captain, the ship is equipped with what appears to be sophisticated weapons. And is protected by an impregnable forcefield," Hawk's AI finally informed him.

Chapter 3

A question of survival

Captain Turner immediately hit the Language and Data Analysis section's icon.

"Yes, Captain, how can I help you?" Language specialist Georgiana Patterson asked.

"Georgiana, transmit the universal-greeting message to that ship in as many languages as possible. Hopefully, someone in that ship might understand enough to decide not to attack us."

"On it, Captain. Can I assume you don't want any pictures or information on origin?"

"Definitely not."

"The ship is getting closer and is starting to move around us," Peter Bracket warned as a zoomable real-time image appeared on the bridge's monitors.

"I reckon they're taking a good look at us," Nick Chambers ventured.

"Captain, I'm detecting micro-pulses across our systems," Bracket informed. "I'm sure they're scanning us."

"We would have anticipated that."

Captain Turner then studied the image and the limited data coming from Hawk's outside sensor grid.

"Anna, is this all the data our sensors can obtain on the Alien ship?"

"Afraid so. We lost three sensor sections when we crashed out of warp," the AI replied.

Turner didn't comment, knowing he should have expected that. Then he hit Georgiana's tab again.

"Georgiana, any response?"

"Nothing, so far."

"Have you tried changing the transmission rate up and down?"

"Of course. But there's still no response."

"Keep at it," Turner ordered while asking himself why he'd queried the obvious. When he knew Georgiana was dedicated and thorough. She certainly didn't need him pressuring her.

Then he tapped Engineering, and Patrick Powers' drawn-looking face appeared on his screen.

"What progress have you made, Patrick?"

"We're replacing the faulty laser coupler as we speak, Captain. So, we should have warp capability in about thirty-five minutes."

"I really hope that's soon enough, Patrick. What about jump readiness?"

"Anna should be able to ascertain jump readiness quicker than me, Captain."

"True, but I need your personal assessment of jump capability."

"Okay," Patrick replied. With that, Turner closed the contact.

Although the alien ship was no longer visible, their tracking sensors had followed the vessel as it slowly moved to the left side of Hawk.

Then Captain Turner concentrated on the view of the alien ship on his main screen.

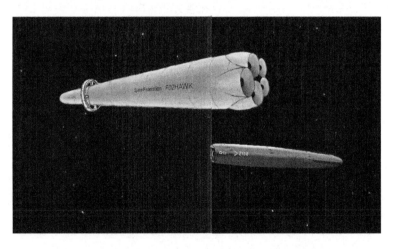

Looking at the ship, Turner felt envious in one respect. This long cigar-shaped vessel with regular blisters across its hull was a massive ship.

'*The blisters are probably its defense system,*' he thought. Then realized that the ship didn't seem to have any jump rings.

"Perhaps they're built-in somehow," Turner speculated out loud.

"At least they've stopped scanning us," Science officer Bracket stated.

"But why bother to move around us? And why face our left side?" Nick Chambers pondered.

"Well, our data analysis and chart room departments are on that side," Bracket pointed out.

"Hell, they can't read our computer streams. Can they?" Turner gasped.

"Maybe… I've seen extra shielding is specified for our next generation of Starships to counter that possibility," Peter Bracket stated.

Then Georgiana interrupted.

"Captain, we've just received a transmission from the alien ship. I'll need time to decipher it, but luckily, it has several anchor words to help us generate a basic language."

"Do what you can, Georgiana. Any progress you make with their language will be good. But I also need you to record and store everything you can on Data crystals. Especially Earth's location, Maps, and anything else that would help the aliens find Earth."

"I assume you are hoping the Aliens won't be able to read the data crystals, Michael?"

26

"Exactly. Once you've done that, you and Anna must delete every reference to Earth on our ship's systems. Then we can recover the information if we survive."

"If we survive?" came her distressed voice.

Turner didn't answer her. He sensed her anguish but had this dark feeling that he couldn't shift.

Five minutes later, the alien ship was much closer and directly facing Hawk. Turner could see what appeared to be a Bridge recessed high up just inside the ship's large circular and flat-shaped front. And he could just make out several beings moving about inside.

In the center of the front face, Turner could also see a large black hole. H'mm, that looks like a tube, which most likely runs deep into the ship's center, he decided.

He zoomed in on the tube section and noted what appeared to be small, greyish-colored rectangular-shaped blocks covering the inside surface of the tube.

"It could be a weapon," Turner speculated out loud.

"Yeah, it looks like a magnetic beam containment tube," Bracket suggested.

"They're scanning us again," Bracket then warned.

"Damn," Turner muttered and tapped Georgiana's personal tab.

"Have you done yet," he asked as her strained-looking face appeared on his screen.

"The crystal recordings are complete. We're now totally erasing all references to Earth from Anna's memory and all the data storage systems," she replied in a croaky-sounding voice.

"Well done," Turner said.

"Are we gonna die, Michael?" She asked.

"I hope not!" He exclaimed. "But I don't know what these aliens are likely to do… We've no real weapons except a meteor deflector system and an inadequate protective screen. So, it's not looking good, Georgie."

With that, Turner reluctantly closed the contact. Then tapped Engineering's icon, and Patrick's image replaced Georgiana's.

"Just six minutes and warp will be available, Captain," Patrick stated.

"Okay. So, we'll jump without priming if we're still around."

"Risky, Captain, but I've seen that ship on the monitors, so I reckon that might be the only way we could jump without being blasted."

"Exactly, Patrick. Initiate the jump immediately. But, through Anna, not through me."

"Understood. But I'll give you the countdown."

Then Patrick was gone, and his image disappeared off Turner's screen. With Mike Ferguson's image replacing it.

Astro's Mike Ferguson uttered a sigh of relief as he reported to Turner.

"Astro's Nav has finally given an approximation to our current location, Captain. Shall we update Earth?"

"No. That will be too dangerous. Just feed the info into the jump control for Procyon."

"Okay."

"They're still scanning us, Captain," Bracket reiterated.

Captain Turner didn't comment as he looked at the corner of his main screen and saw Patrick's jump countdown commence. It registered five minutes twenty-five seconds.

'Come on, come on,' Turner desperately urged, mentally trying to speed it up.

Then his heart missed a beat as the small greyish rectangular blocks covering the whole of the tube's inner surface turned red.

"No," Turner gasped as he saw a pale blue ball of fire flash out of the alien's central tube.

He felt Hawk shudder, and as he looked on, he saw a large section of Hawk's hull vaporize.

Then came a moment of searing heat, and the ship's power instantly ceased.

Turner struggled as air rapidly left the vessel and cold invaded his body. Then his mind went blank as frost started to permeate throughout the ship.

All life on board Hawk finally ceased.

Chapter 4

Did that really happen?

Frank Richardson's Heavy-Cruiser, Capri, exited hyperspace almost on top of a sizeable *Aarcat* warship. With Capri's collision alarms sounding.

"Weapons and shield power grids online in three seconds," yelled Lieutenant Busby.

"She's going to warp," Lieutenant Morrison frantically warned, seeing the alien ship's warp pulse forming.

"Back us out of here…. Now," Frank yelled.

"Weapons and shield online," Busby confirmed as his board indicated the emitter doors had opened, and the particle beam collimators were extended.

"Well, fire at the damn thing before it jumps and takes us with it," Frank snapped.

The Capri jerked backward under full thrust while its forward cannon opened fire. But the *Aarcat* warship continued elongating, then slid forward into its wormhole and safety.

The Capri rocked as the Aarcat warship's warp field rippled space-time for a few seconds before collapsing. Then the ripples disappeared, and stability quickly returned to Capri.

Frank wasn't sure why a single *Aarcat* warship would have turned up on its own. Even though it was true that, since the Aarcat race had attacked and virtually wiped out all of Earth's outposts, earth forces had suffered setback after setback. And now, a scout ship had reported that a fleet of nine major Aarcat warships had entered the Sol system and was heading for Earth.

Frank could feel his crew's despair in knowing that Capri was the only ship available to block the alien's advance. And the inevitable destruction of Earth and their families was only too plain to see.

"The Aarcat fleet will be here in…, four minutes 38 seconds," Lieutenant Morrison warned.

"Where the hell are the rest of our ships?" Frank grumbled.

Then Earth's Battleship Vanguard and another Heavy Cruiser, Victory, dropped out of warp to Capri's right.

Frank groaned. He couldn't believe that just two ships had been sent to help Capri thwart a group of nine *Aarcat* warships. And more importantly, the warships were just minutes away from beating the hell out of them.

Just then, the voice of the Vanguards Fleet Commander came through the ship-to-ship comms.

"I am Fleet Commander Banning. I know what you are thinking, Captain. But ours are the only ships available to you," Banning stated.

"Understood. But the Aarcat ships will be on us in four minutes," Frank warned him, knowing that it could only end one way with just three ships against nine.

"So, I can see," Banning agreed. "There's nothing I can do about it. The rest of our ships are gone.... Ambushed. And the crews slaughtered like vermin," Banning added in a strained-sounding voice.

"Then we'll take as many of the Aliens with us as possible," Frank coldly stated.

"Agreed."

"We could just jump and hit the sods closer to Earth," Frank suggested. "Or better still, conduct guerrilla warfare," he added.

"No, Captain. We stand and fight," Banning ordered. "Earth is as good as gone."

Frank groaned to himself. He knew there were very few crew members on ships these days. Even so, he reckoned they would have had a better chance of inflicting damage using hit-and-run tactics. While saving human lives. But unfortunately, he was not in command.

"Two minutes," Lieutenant Morrison interjected.

"Good luck, everyone... See you on the other side," came Tanner's last words.

"Screens to max," Frank ordered.

"Weapons ready to lock as soon as they're in range," Lieutenant Busby confirmed.

Then Frank sat back and waited for the inevitable to happen.

The Aarcat race had overwhelmed Earth's outposts, and Earth forces had suffered setback after setback. But, even now, no one knew where the species had originated.

The Aarcat's tactic was to attack in groups of nine ships in a flat-plate head-on configuration. Thus, ensuring the group's overall firepower simply overwhelmed the force in front of them. This tactic had been highly successful, with Earth losing most of its capital ships by this method.

The nine Aarcat warships suddenly came to a halt, directly in front of the Earth ships and in the expected configuration.

"Wait," Frank yelled.

Nothing happened for a moment. Then the Battleship Vanguard, and Heavy Cruiser Victory, opened fire on the middle Aarcat ship, which they had assumed would be the command ship.

"Don't fire yet," Frank forcefully ordered Capri's, Lieutenant Busby.

"Captain...?"

Having listened to all three Earth ships running commentaries and their chatter via his Command console, Frank finally snapped, "Wait."

Then the Aarcat ships returned fire, with devastating effect.

Particle beams tore through Vanguard's protective screen, and her hull rippled and melted from the onslaught. Then Frank heard Vanguard's Captain's death scream as he and his crew vaporized in a ball of fire.

Then, multiple explosions shattered Vanguard's weapon's energy-containment spheres. Sending a vortex of fire that melted bulkheads throughout the ship as it went.

Frank felt sick as the Capri shuddered from the shock wave. And he saw Vanguard break apart and slowly tumble in space while venting smoke and debris from the still-hot ruptures along one side of her twisted hull.

"Captain, why are we just sitting here?" Lieutenant Busby angrily queried, noting Frank's reluctance to engage the Alien ships.

Frank didn't reply.

Another explosion rocked Capri, pushing her violently sideways as Victory's warp core exploded and blew her apart. Then glowing gases permeated a few segments of the heavy cruiser's hull, and her broken metal skeleton slowly dispersed.

While multiple pieces of debris drifted along, further out in space.

Lieutenant Morrison took a few seconds to stabilize the Capri. Then the weapon's systems came back online.

"Lieutenant Busby, concentrate all weapons fire on the far left ship," Frank ordered.

"Lieutenant Morrison, swing outward, Full sub, straight at that outer ship." Then added, "The other ships won't be able to hit us."

"About time," Busby muttered as Capri surged forward with her weapons hot.

Just then, Capri's collision alarm sounded.

"What… where is it?" Frank called out in disbelief.

"Bloody hell Captain, it's a chunk of Victory's hull, and it's coming…."

Lieutenant Morrison never finished what he was saying.

And Capri shuddered as a segment of Victory's hull crashed into Capri. Violently tearing off the ship's front, leaving Frank seated in his command chair, totally alone. Luckily, his seat's emergency survival force field temporarily protected him from death.

Frank was shaken by the trauma and unsure of how he could be looking out into space through a gigantic hole yet still be alive.

Then he shivered as an alien entity resembling an oversized octopus glided through the hole and stopped in front of him. Frank noticed a bluish glow around the entity and knew it had to be some sort of spacesuit.

The Alien seemed to study him for a moment. Then it slowly extended two of its tentacles, which passed through the seat's force field and started encircling Frank's body.

"Murderers," Frank managed to shout at it before blackness filled his mind....

The Holo movie suddenly ended, and Frank's adrenalin rush slowly dropped, leaving him drained by the frantic interactive action he'd gone through.

A prompt appeared on the small menu screen at hand.

'To continue, place your debit disc on the scanner and select another ending.'

"Damn," Frank shouted, realizing he should have selected one of the specialist endings offered at the start of the interactive movie, like Guerilla warfare.

But he decided to call it a day. However, he was impressed that he knew the crew and ship's names without them being pushed in his face and spoiling the experience. I guess it must be a subliminal thing, he decided.

Although this Holo system wasn't new, the advancement in interactive holo projectors had been rapid over the last few years and, once experienced, never forgotten.

The Holo projection system cost more than the average household could afford, so hundreds of micro cinemas had sprung up across many cities. These catered to small groups or individuals desiring a form of escapism from the drudgery of everyday life, with the Holo projector sensing the viewing participant's face and directing the desired movie action toward it, with the latter feeling more involved in the action.

Frank took the supposedly free alcohol drink from the robot attendant at his seat. Then drank it slowly to extend the session time. Knowing that the 'drink time' was built into the Cinema's exorbitant charge for a single-person session. Then ignored the request to leave a tip when he left the microcinema.

Once outside, Frank checked the time and was surprised to see that it was already just after three in the afternoon, and he'd spent nearly four hours in combat.

As Frank approached the closest waiting Mag cab, its door automatically slid open. Once inside, the door closed, and Frank instructed the Cab's administrator to take him to his apartment in Hampstead.

Lights on the front panel in front of Frank flipped between Red and Green. Stopped on Green, and a destination map illuminated, showing a Transit time of 18 minutes. The Cab moved away and followed the old underground locator link with the city's computer system. These locators automatically juggled the traffic to allow Cabs a safe and swift passage.

Once Frank arrived at his apartment, he paid with his Debit disc, then ordered the Mag taxi for eight-thirty the following morning.

After a good night's sleep and a decent breakfast, Frank prepared for his next seven-day shift. He packed all he needed into a special case supplied by the Space Federation, and the case's lid hissed as it shut and sealed.

Then Frank's wrist pad bleeped, and the words, *Cab waiting'* appeared on it, and he hurriedly locked up his apartment and left.

The MAG cab's sliding door opened as he approached and slid in. "Knightsbridge central," he directed the cab as it set off.

From Knightsbridge central, Frank would take the high-speed Magnetic-levitation train to Area 16 at London's Spaceport hub.

Frank relaxed as the Taxi sped on towards Knightsbridge central. Even so, he knew the next seven days would certainly be a letdown after yesterday's Holo Cinema excitement.

He was, nevertheless, eager to be heading back into space.

Chapter 5

One year earlier

Earth, 2300, A.D

November the 17th

The two medium-range 'Sling' transporters, Reliant and Albury, were in a geostationary orbit 460 kilometers above the Kennedy Space Center.

Captain Frank Richardson stared impatiently through the pilot's forward window in the Reliant as the Earth shuttle curved slowly up and towards them. It was scheduled to dock with them in eight minutes.

Although Reliant's flight deck was small compared to the Earth Shuttle's. Frank's and the engineering departments' stations each had a bank of five virtual monitors. The large centrally placed virtual display on the technician's ops station switched between twenty cameras around the Reliant's outer hull. While at the same time, Frank's primary monitor covered the

41

pilot's forward and rear views. At the back of the flight deck were two spare anti-inertia seats.

The two medium-range Sling Transporters were designed to attach to the new crewless *Fast Carrier* vessels, which could reach point five three lightspeed. Thus, the transit time to Mars was cut to about four point five minutes, not counting the build-up and longer stopping times.

The Reliant and Albury were scheduled to arrive at Mars in about two hours, depending on Mars's orbital position.

While Frank waited for the shuttle to dock and its two high-ranking Spacefed personnel to board, he thought about Paula.

Frank was just nineteen when he graduated from Uni and went straight into a Mag-Train supervisor's position at Speedex's HQ, where he met Paula. And, as their friendship developed, he became noticeably confident, with a growing lust for life showing in everything he did.

Then tragedy struck. Paula and his parents died in a freak accident when the fuel cell in the vehicle they were traveling in short-circuited and exploded.

After that, Frank suffered tremendous grief and despair over the tragic death of Paula and his parents. And lost his way. More than a year passed before he recovered enough to join the SpaceFed pilot training scheme.

This was the turning point for Frank. He passed his primary Pilot training with flying colors and continued his training with *Warbend Elite* and on a specialist private course in coping with and counteracting unforeseen space-related problems.

These included inherent forcefield weaknesses and things that Spacefed didn't explain about warp-core theory.

Now, at 36, Frank had fully developed physically and mentally. And, with his darkish hair and piercing blue eyes, he had that bit of a 'gung-ho' attitude about him.

The ship-to-ship intercom bleeped, bringing Frank back to the present.

"Albury's confirmed her ready status, Frank," his engineer cum dogs-body Johnny reported.

"Ok. Sync with Albury and ensure we are set to link up with our Fast Carriers. In…, twelve minutes," Frank stated, having checked the countdown.

"Oh. And make sure our VIPs are secured in their seats as soon as they are aboard."

"As always, Frank," Johnny replied.

It was common knowledge that Frank preferred a more relaxed command attitude. In fact, he had always got more out of people when on first-name terms. Though he would insist on the use of his Captain's title when needed.

Frank got on well with Johnny Stern. He was twenty-eight, very conscientious, and respected Frank's intuitions, even though they had been somewhat riskier of late.

Frank watched Johnny raise the artificial gravity to 0.5 of Earth's for the VIPs. Then Johnny left his console and headed for the main airlock.

Although everyone on board had magnets in their foot-ware to help keep their feet on the floor, a crude version of a gravity generator operated when VIPs were on board.

Frank glanced at his secondary screen as it showed the two high-ranking Spacefed personnel settling in.

He had already familiarized himself with his two VIPs, Jack Medcalf, head of the U.K. section of the Space Federation, and Director Mertoff of the Russian arm.

He knew they were in their fifties with similar physical attributes and hair coloring, apart from Mertoff's mustache and grey eyes. And both were dressed in dark blue Spacefed Upper-Rank uniforms, with an emblem showing a Starship across a star-studded background on each shoulder.

Once Frank had verified Albury's status, he contacted her Captain, Stuart Rankin.

"Our carriers will be here in eleven minutes," Stuart volunteered on seeing Frank's face on his Comms screen.

"So, I see. But from what I can also see on my security panel, this cargo of yours appears to have a weird security flag."

"The cargo is the final Core for the Andromeda. And the flag means Protect at all costs."

"Then we'd better keep our intership Data-link open, just in case, Stuart."

"Agreed."

Frank closed the visual link to Rankin and relaxed, noting that Johnny was now waiting at the airlock. Then, not seeing anything urgent showing on his monitors or the consoles, he shut his eyes for a moment.

Frank awoke to a buzzing sound and a stinging sensation on the back of his neck, making him sweat.

"Damn," he muttered while noting that both VIPs were already in their designated anti-inertia seats. And Johnny was back at his station.

"Are you alright, Frank," Johnny asked, seeing bewilderment on Frank's face.

"Yes," he replied after checking for malfunctions or changes on his console. But there were none that he could see.

"Johnny, check to see if insects came in with our two passengers."

Johnny quickly checked the internal scanners and filters.

"Nothing registers, Frank."

"Weird."

"Uh, there is one thing, though. Our ship's clock shows a minus two-minute time discrepancy with Earth's time-sync transmitter."

"How is that possible?"

"Not sure. I'll check it anyway. But if I temporarily reset our master clock. It shouldn't affect our link-up with the Fast Carrier."

"Then do it," Frank ordered, realizing the patch on his neck felt sore.

"Done," Johnny confirmed. As the two Fast Carrier units came to a halt. One of them sitting above the Reliant and the other above the Albury.

Both Sling transporter vessels moved upward to automatically dock with their designated carriers via Reliant's and Albury's curved claw-like locking arms. The arms had automatic docking sensors at their ends that contacted with the Carriers locking mechanisms.

"Capture lock, secured," Johnny informed. "Two minutes to engage."

Frank left his seat and virtually glided along into the higher-gravity passenger department.

"We'll be off in about two minutes," he informed his VIPs. "We should arrive just outside Mars's exclusion zone in two hours, eleven minutes, but I'll keep you updated. The service Droid will supply you with any refreshments you want."

Both nodded without looking up from their operations pads.

Frank felt slightly hurt by their evident dismissal, as he returned to the pilot's seat. Then readied himself for the next thirty-two minutes of exhilarating acceleration to enable their group of ships to reach point five three light-speed.

The group countdown started…. Five…, Four…, Three…, Two…, One…, Zero."

Then the Fast Carriers jerked forward as their massive drive engines went to full power. Frank sank back in his inertia-dampening seat, gritting his teeth while enjoying every moment.

Chapter 6

Disaster

In the meantime, no reason had been found for the time discrepancy. Or for how Frank got stung on the back of his neck.

Thirty-two minutes later, the Reliant and Albury group reached their maximum speed of point five-three of light. They would stay at this speed for another five minutes, then start their ninety-minute deceleration before coming to a halt close to Mars.

Frank and Johnny continued their inflight monitoring and the preparations for docking at the Mars orbital shipyards. But Frank couldn't stop himself from deliberately turning on his passenger area's surveillance camera for a while.

He noted that both VIPs were still using Reliant's sub-space link. And, seeing that they were totally engrossed, wondered what they were up to.

After an uneventful trip, both groups finally halted just outside the Mars exclusion zone.

The locking arms disengaged, and the Fast Carrier vessels moved clear of the Sling transporters.

Then the Comms came alive.

"Mars control to Reliant and Albury. You may enter the exclusion zone. Flightpath and docking access data are now in your Actions Nav. Note that you will not be able to deviate from this path. Keep your Comms open for this maneuver."

"Acknowledged, Control. We are proceeding to Mars Dock," Frank replied.

Then he and Johnny tapped in their control protocols and corrections, and both Reliant and Albury started to accelerate towards Mars.

Almost immediately, there was a flash from the other side of Mars, and the comms died.

"Is it us?" Frank asked Johnny.

A few seconds later, "I can't locate any problems with us. So, it must be Mars," Johnny answered, just as their Comms came back to life.

"Mars control to Reliant and Albury. Do not execute your docking. Stay there."

"Why?" Johnny involuntarily asked Control.

"The crewless test ship, *Explorer*, has exited warp too close to Mars' surface and disintegrated. Some of its debris has been blown into space."

"Are we in danger?"

"Be alert. We are chasing down sections of the Explorer where their trajectory has been *bent* your way."

"And the Mars facility?"

"Surface and space facilities seem safe right now. However, the resultant EMP pulse has locked Albury to the station. I repeat, stay where you are until further notice."

With that, the conversation ended.

"So, they haven't detected that we are already moving," Frank muttered.

Albury's collision alarm suddenly sounded throughout Reliant's flight deck as something clanged against the ship, then rolled over the top of Reliant's hull, startling them.

Frank and Johnny checked their monitors and could see debris tumbling in space while smoke and flames billowed out from a gouge in the Albury's hull.

Then the voice of Albury's Captain Rankin rattled across the ship-to-ship Comms.

"Frank," Rankin's anxious-sounding voice blurted out. "We've lost all primary thruster and maneuverability power."

"Captain Rankin. Can you confirm which sensors are working?" Johnny asked. "We're not getting all the status updates from your net," he explained.

"A few, like the forward camera and range sensors," Rankin replied, then paused briefly.

"We may appear dead in the water, but our forward momentum will be a killer," Rankin added. Then, paused again as he tried to compose himself.

"Life support has kicked in, but we have started to pitch and roll, with some yaw thrown in. I don't have any more info. Besides, just before the hit, Nav confirmed we were correctly locked on the shipyard's Homing Beacon." Rankin paused again, then continued.

"So, we can't stop Albury's independent Ion thrusters keeping us on course to hit the Spacedock facility," Rankin warned, then waited, but no one answered.

"H'mm, the homing beacon is a fail-safe to stop ships wandering off-course," Mertoff remarked, then realized the implications.

"Then the homing beacon system is flawed, Mertoff," Frank interjected.

"Where's Marcus?" Frank then asked Rankin.

"He's gone to check the cargo."

"Captain Rankin, you've got to save your cargo at all costs," came the panicky voice of Director Mertoff, now standing behind Johnny.

"What with, Director?" came Rankin's question, his voice sounding strained.

"We'll get back to you, Rankin," Frank assured him.

"There's no way a Mars Tug could reach Albury in time, let alone lock onto the ship," Johnny stated. "I see Albury's wobbling as well," he added.

"Noted. Anyway, we'd be too close to Mars by then for a Tug to do anything," Frank acknowledged.

Then Captain Rankin called in again. "Marcus says the cargo seems to have activated its own power source and looks safe for the moment."

"That's good news, Captain."

Frank selected Manual and started moving Reliant closer to Albury, then felt a hand gently grip his shoulder as Jack Medcalf whispered in his ear.

"There's got to be a way, Frank. Losing Albury and its cargo will put Andromeda and the other ships back at least three years."

It was strange, but Frank felt he had known Jack Medcalf forever. And realized that Jack understood the danger and the need for a miracle better than Mertoff.

"Get on with it," Mertoff growled, urging Frank on.

Frank turned to him. "Director. Sit down and keep out of our way, or I'll throw you in the Brig, myself."

"Come on, Mertoff," Jack urged. "Sit down with me. They need to concentrate."

"Bah... Put a couple of Droids with thrusters on Albury's hull. That will do the trick."

Frank made an aggressive gesture as if to get up.

"Alright... Sorry, Captain. I know I'm prone to speaking without thinking," Mertoff muttered.

Frank didn't bother to reply.

Then Frank and Johnny turned their attention back to the Albury, just five hundred meters away.

They noted that the damaged rear section holding the thruster control was intermittently visible as the Albury slowly rolled. And the yaw element was making it impossible to lock onto anything.

"Captain, there's surely no way we can sync with Albury with that amount of variation?" Johnny queried.

"I'm not sure about that, but I've got to try."

"Just make sure you don't kill us as well, Frank."

"I'll try not to," Frank replied as he opened the contact with Captain Rankin again and briefly explained what they were about to attempt.

"Lock yourselves in, folks. We're about to commit a version of Hari Kari."

"What are you thinking, Frank?" Jack asked as they all secured themselves in their anti-inertia seats.

"See here," Frank said, pointing to the screen. "The curved locking arm has a meter half-circular cutout on its leading-edge.... So, if I can flip Reliant. Then sync with Albury's rotation and manage to mate with her locking arm. We can use our thrusters to arrest her forward motion, then the Mars tugs can bring her in," Frank finished.

"Christ, Frank. Are you mad? You'll kill us all," Johnny exclaimed in horror.

Chapter 7

The edge of Death

Then Frank contacted Albury's Captain to tell him exactly what they would attempt.

"Captain Rankin, when we flip, we will be flying backward with no real-time visuals of the distancing from Mars. So, we will need you to be our eyes," he explained.

"Frank, this is madness. Think about it. It's unpredictable," Johnny reiterated.

"It has to be worth a try, Johnny," Jack Medcalf interjected.

"Yes, that seems to be the only way open to us," Mertoff added.

"Agreed," Rankin stated. "We have got to stop Albury from hitting the Spacedock facility."

"Captain, I can set up a direct link with Reliant's Nav. Then they could access it on their own Vis," Albury's engineer Mark suggested.

"Excellent, set it up, Marcus," Rankin ordered him.

"Johnny, am I right in thinking that the standard Ion thrusters have a zero-motion shutdown safeguard?"

"Yes, Frank. They will auto-shutdown if we manage to halt Albury's forward motion."

"Excellent, that's what I was hoping for," Frank replied.

Okay, the more we debate, the less time I will have to lock on. So, here we go," Frank said as he touched the virtual display menu's flip tab.

Almost instantly, they could see the Reliant's maneuvering thrusters start to flip the ship 180 degrees.

Once they were flying backward, Frank hit the manual tab, and a two-handed control column extended out from his console.

"Johnny. Give me some figures."

"Albury's navigation feed places Mars at 2,240 Km. With the space docks at just 1,920 Km," Johnny confirmed, sounding worried.

"So, that means, at our group speed of 568 Km per hour, we'll impact with the shipyard in two hours twenty-one minutes," Johnny concluded.

"What info have we got on Albury's rotational speed and yaw element?"

"I reckon she's rotating at one-point twenty-one meters per second, Frank. But the yaw factor is difficult to predict, at about six degrees max."

Frank studied Albury's movement until his plan of action was clear in his mind. And he was sure he could throw the Reliant around fast enough, and accurately enough, to contact with Albury's curved locking arm.

"Right, no unhelpful chatter," he ordered, aiming his comment at Mertoff.

"Ok, Captain Rankin, we are going to try. Now," Frank warned the Albury.

Still five hundred meters from Albury, the Reliant started its long and dangerous backward and upside-down approach to Albury's undulating hull.

"Impact in two hours, nine minutes," Johnny advised.

"Geeze, Johnny. Just overlay the distance on my screen instead of interrupting me."

"Done, Frank. Ok, less distraction, everyone," Johnny said, emphasizing Frank's point.

No one spoke as the distance between the two locking arms slowly clicked, down.

Over the next few minutes, Frank, aware that Mars had already grown appreciably larger on their screens, eased Reliant closer to Albury in a series of short maneuvering bursts.

Frank knew there was no margin for error. He only had one chance to get it right before Albury would otherwise crash into the space dock if he missed the locking arms contact.

Frank kept the Reliant safely away from Albury's locking arm and concentrated on matching Albury's rotational speed. But he found it draining, flying backward and upside down with reference to Albury's position. Even so, he was slowly getting there.

Ten minutes passed before Frank finally matched Albury's rotation. Then his main screen showed both Albury and Reliant's curved locking arms. With the continually changing distance between them over-laid on the screen.

Albury's arm was just meters from Reliant's hull at her extreme yaw point. So, as the yawing Albury moved rapidly away, Frank forced the Reliant to follow. Then made a rapid retreat again, as the arm came swinging back like some massive hammer.

Frank fine-tuned his dangerous operation by closing the separation time. This in-and-out action was repeated several times.

Then suddenly, Albury's curved docking arm's half-moon cutout was just in front of Reliant's cutout.

A gasp came from behind as Frank made his next move. And Reliant's forward right-hand and rear right-hand thrusters fired, jerking Reliant around enough to get an angle on Albury's cutout.

Then Frank moved the control column to maximum forward drive in a continuous flow, and the Reliant tried to surge forward. But the main drive kept running.

Then the ship shuddered, and crunching metal sounded through both ships.

More gasps came from behind him as the closing distance between the Albury and the shipyard started to slow.

Another sound of groaning metal rumbled as the two twisting ship hulls briefly came into contact.

"We're almost there," Frank stated, using Reliant's side thrusters to keep the ships safely apart.

While both transporters' forward motion slowly came to a halt. And Reliant's main drive instantly dropped power to equal Albury's thrusters, just long enough to cause Albury's motion sensor to shut down her own thrusters.

Then, silence reigned once more.

Johnny grabbed Frank's hand and shook it. "Genius, Frank. Genius."

"Tiring, that's for sure," Frank stated as he slumped back in his seat, exhausted.

"Albury's Ion thrusters have shut down," Johnny confirmed, smiling.

"Thank goodness."

"Well done, Frank," came Jack and Mertoff's congratulations as they patted him on his shoulder.

Then Captain Rankin's voice erupted from the comms. "A master class in thinking outside the box, Frank."

"Thanks," Frank acknowledged and sat back momentarily before deciding to separate the ships.

Once clear, Frank used the maneuvering thrusters to flip his ship 180 degrees. A short, braking-thruster burst and Reliant quickly separated from Albury.

Mars was directly in front of both ships now, and they
were only 988 Kms from the space docks.

Although the image of Mars almost filled the flight deck's windows, the multi-unit spacedock and the ships moored to it stood out in vivid detail against the curving horizon.

"Makes you proud to be human," Frank remarked as he took in the magnitude of the Facility.

"What's that ship, Mert?" Jack queried, pointing to a small gray, blunt-nosed ship moored near Andromeda.

"It's a bit like Albury, but it's more likely to be a small military ship," Johnny interjected.

Mertoff agreed as the Mars Comms link suddenly burst into life.

"Mars control to Reliant and Albury. Well, done," came the congratulations. But Frank could hear some sort of confusion in the background.

"Is everything alright there," he queried.

"Yes," came a different, and stressed-sounding voice.

"A tug will be with Albury to take it to Andromeda's loading bay in twenty minutes, Captain Richardson. And, as originally scheduled, you may bring Reliant in and dock at Andromeda's forward airlock."

"Understood," Frank acknowledged as if nothing was worrying him.

With that, the transmission ended.

Then Frank called Captain Rankin on a secure inter ship channel.

"I've got a bad feeling about this, Rankin."

"Me too," came Rankin's immediate response.

"Just do everything asked and get your cargo on board Andromeda as fast as possible," Frank urged.

"I intend to do that… What about you, Frank?"

"The same. But we will have to play it by ear," Frank cautiously replied. "Have you any weapons?"

"None at all. Apparently, weapons have been deemed a risk to our cargo."

"Shame. Okay, we'll see you on Andromeda." With that, Frank closed contact with Albury.

"Frank, take your time," Jack advised. "Mertoff and I have things to discuss before we dock."

"My thoughts exactly," Frank agreed.

After Jack and Mertoff returned to the passenger's section, Frank noted that the hyperlink usage warning had activated.

He then over-rode the only permitted docking variable and adjusted the Reliant's forward speed to ensure that it would be an hour before they docked with Andromeda.

Then Frank turned his attention to the Mars spacedock complex and studied it in more detail with Johnny.

"Do we have any weapons on board other than those in the cabinet?" Frank asked.

"As far as I know, just what's in the cabinet, Frank."

"What about the cargo destined for Andromeda?"

Johnny brought up the shipment itinerary on his screen. "Just fitness and general items…. Wait a minute."

"What is it?"

"This is different," Johnny said as he interrogated the manifest in depth. "A particle beam weapon…. A large one, at that."

"Take a Droid and see if you can get it out and power it up."

"Okay, but we could be done over this," Johnny warned Frank.

"I shouldn't worry about that, Johnny. Anyway, I'll link you to my comms so you can keep up to speed with what's happening."

Johnny then went off to the rear cargo hold. While Frank waited until the Hyperlink was deactivated before joining Jack and Mertoff.

"All right, you two, what gives with this military ship?" He asked the pair as he sat down opposite them.

"Just a certain Commodore Winton, flexing his muscles," Jack replied.

"Yes, but we'll come to that in a while, Frank," Mertoff irritably stated.

"Okay," Frank replied while wondering what was upsetting Mertoff.

"Carter, Andromeda's prospective Captain, has decided against accepting the position," Mertoff told him.

"Why would Carter give up such a fantastic position?" Frank asked.

"The Transceiver…," Mertoff started to say.

"Let me explain, Frank," Jack said, interrupting Mertoff.

"This transceiver is experimental… I'm not qualified to go into detail. Still, it's apparently inserted in the brain where the brain's Axon connections are particularly dense.

Over time, the insert's filaments will meld with the user's brain functions. And this would inevitably make the brain a part of Andromeda's High-brain."

Jack explained. "You can imagine the operational benefits this would give the user," he added.

"Okay, so, what was Carter's problem?" Frank asked.

"The Transceiver can be turned off but never removed."

Frank thought about this for a while. While Mertoff and Jack looked at each other, then Mertoff nodded an okay to Jack.

"Because Carter changed his mind, Frank, and after checking you out, we decided you would be a perfect choice for the position," Jack said, then paused briefly.

"Especially with what you did to save Albury. Everything tells us that you have all we could wish to be appointed Andromeda's Captain," Jack stated as he looked hopefully at Frank.

"Well, if you can turn it off, I guess I could live with that," Frank said, having thought it over.

"Excellent," Jack stated. Then stopped and glanced briefly at Mertoff before adding.

"We know you don't have a family, Frank...., and I would be happy to take you under my wing. So, come and live with my wife and me until Andromeda is ready to start her acceptance trials."

"Really?"

"Yes, really, Frank. Georgina would love to have another man about the house."

"That's a very generous offer, Jack," Frank said and mulled it over.

"In that case, I would be honored to take the position. If Spacefed sanctions it."

"They just have, Frank. Welcome aboard, son."

Chapter 8

Dangerous Liaison

"So, this Commodore Winton. Why have they allowed his military ship to be out here?" Frank then asked.

"Well, even though the military's presence in space was banned before the Space Federation came into being in 2235, Winton has visions of grandeur," Mertoff cynically stated.

"Yes. And we all know the military is still operating in space. They even have a space station," Frank pointed out.

"Agreed. And the Earth Federation appears to have turned a blind eye to the fact that the military has already put out civilian contracts to build two massive ships," Jack stated.

"Even so, whatever we think a Space Navy will come into fruition at some point," Mertoff pointed out.

"Okay. Let's move on," Frank urged after a couple of minutes, knowing that time was running out, and he would soon have to be back on Reliant's flight deck.

"So, Mertoff. I feel you know what that military ship really is, don't you?"

"Perhaps. A year ago, I know it was simply a type of shuttle servicing the military station."

"But the ship's too far out for that, Mertoff," Jack interjected.

"Then it must have been upgraded. I briefly saw the ship's specifications on my pad before security removed the specs. And, if I remember correctly, it has a pilot and five personnel who are probably marines."

"Then, we definitely need to see a schematic of that ship," Frank said. "You must have some contacts, Director Mertoff?" he prompted.

Mertoff didn't reply straight away.

"Yes…, and I know exactly who to call. I will contact Director Tompkin in the states. He'll know," Mertoff confirmed.

Then added in an aside, "You might as well call me Mert, Frank. Seeing as we are going to be together for a while.

Then, Mertoff called Tompkin on a secure Hyper-link channel and explained their dilemma.

Moments later, Frank heard a bleep confirming the schematics had been received. And his central virtual screen would shortly display a complete schematic of the Military ship.

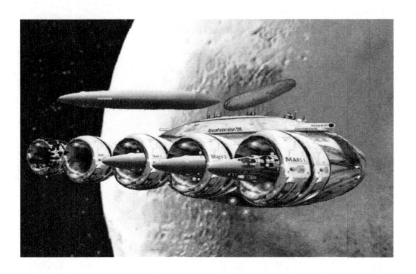

"Follow me," Frank ordered as he got up and headed for the flight deck, with Jack and Mertoff following close behind.

They could see Mars almost filling the flight deck's windows as they entered. With the spacedock between their ship and Mars and the small blunt-nosed ship still moored near Andromeda.

Frank looked at the central virtual screen and saw that a message had been embedded with the schematics.

The message said it all. *'Assume military ship is hostile.'*

Frank looked at the screen again and noted that the docking-time count-down showed twenty-one minutes remaining.

Then Frank rotated the schematic image of the Military ship on the virtual display to match the moored military vessel.

"H'mm, virtually the same," Frank muttered as he zoomed in closer. Then shifted his view from the military vessel to Andromeda and back again.

A plan was forming in Frank's mind. But it depended on three factors.

One, whether Johnny could get the Particle Beam weapon out?

Two. Would the beam weapon have sufficient backup power to enable it to fire?

Three. Having noted the other vessel's angle and exactly where Reliant would dock with Andromeda's forward airlock. Would these factors really make his plan viable?

Even if they did, there was one more thing Frank had to be sure of, so he selected Mars control.

"Reliant to Mars control. Confirm the docking protocol," Frank requested.

"Docking procedure is correct. Nineteen minutes to docking clamp," came a male-sounding voice.

"Are there any unwanted repercussions expected from Explorer? Or with the Military ship being close to Andromeda?" Frank then asked.

There was an overly long pause before the operator replied.

"From Explorer, no Captain. But there is a new control setup, Xc7.

Please dock safely," the operator advised him.

The link then closed.

Frank quickly tapped in Xc7, and a hidden message was displayed.

"Well, whoever you are, you've been on the same course as me," Frank exclaimed as he and his two VIPs finished reading it.

Then he updated Johnny.

"Okay, the Mars Controller says he has one marine with him in comms and four on Andromeda. But the pilot is staying on the military ship," Frank stated.

Then added, "Johnny, we need to dock at the left airlock and facing aft."

Frank felt under pressure, noting that the docking time read just nineteen minutes. But he lightened up when Johnny came back to the flight deck.

"It's all good, Frank," Johnny reported while acknowledging the other two.

"We are mounting the Particle Beam weapon just outside the right airlock and facing forward."

"You must have been reading my mind," Frank joked.

"I listened and put myself in your shoes, Frank," Johnny simply replied.

"It's PCC registers just over a giga-joule, but its backup power cell only has enough power for one shot," he warned.

"The downside is that our Droid won't fire at the military ship because there's a human on board."

"Noted. Okay, can you fire the beam weapon from here, Johnny?" Frank asked.

"Yes. It's mounted in a gimbal, so I should be able to direct the beam."

"Good. Okay, we've got fifteen minutes."

"We need to act as if nothing is wrong," Jack warned.

Mertoff agreed.

"Johnny. You'll be staying on board. So, when I say *Jungle Beat*, fire at the military ship. Make sure you hit it at the same point Albury was hit."

"That won't be a problem, Frank."

"Has the cell enough power?" Mertoff queried.

"It's rated at two giga-joules," Johnny reassured him.

"Yes, but we'll be limited to one giga-joule, which will have to be enough," Frank interjected. "Just as you said, Johnny."

Frank quickly re-checked Andromeda's basic specs in case he'd missed something that could jeopardize his plan.

Even though work on Andromeda was still going on, her basic operations and life support systems were now fully operational.

She was oval-shaped, a kilometer-long and one hundred meters in diameter at her widest, with each end tapering almost to a point.

He knew the rear section was at risk and that this section was a slightly darker shade than the rest of the ship. And was made from a material that enabled the steerable, specially bonded photonic laser stream to pass through unhindered.

More importantly, the beam needed to hit the military ship, not Andromeda.

Frank was also pleased that the force field emitters embedded around her hull at regular intervals, and showing as tiny blisters, would not be in Johnny's line of fire.

"Okay, we're good," Frank finally muttered to himself.

Seeing that Reliant had already started on its pre-programmed path to dock with Andromeda's forward airlock. Frank collected two small handheld Beamers and four micro ear-transceivers from the weapons cabinet. Then handed the three of them a transceiver while putting the other one in his front pocket, saying, "We'll need these to talk to each other."

Frank then tucked one beamer out of sight behind his back and the other in a side pocket.

"What about us?" Jack queried, not seeing any weapons for them.

"It's better that you don't have any. Just concentrate on Andromeda and ignore me completely."

"Where are we going to meet after?" Mertoff asked.

"Both of you come back here. Johnny, let me know when everyone's back on board. And set up a carrier link-up for four hours from when we board Andromeda."

"You'd better make sure you get back, Frank," Johnny insisted.

"I will."

Once they had inserted their ear transceivers and checked that all links were working correctly, they got ready to leave the Reliant.

No one spoke as they waited at the inner airlock for the external force-field technology transfer tube to establish.

Once established, the green-colored *'Airtight'* light illuminated, signaling no air was escaping around the transfer tube's seal.

Then the Reliant's airlock doors opened, and Frank stepped inside the shimmering transfer tube together with Jack and Mertoff. Then they drifted across the tube and into Andromeda's open airlock.

A single marine Sargent, dressed in light body armor, nervously greeted them as they stepped into the low-gravity zone in Andromeda's reception area, which linked to her central corridor.

"No weapons allowed on board," the Sargent forcefully ordered.

"You two go on. I have work to do here first," Frank said as he took the beam weapon from his pocket and held it out to the marine.

Jack and Mert took the hint, sidestepped, and hurried off and out of immediate danger.

"Wait," the surprised marine called after them.

"Here." Frank forcefully snapped, and the marine's attention jerked back to him. He took Frank's weapon as an angry-looking, lightly armored marine captain approached them.

"Sargent Stewart, you know that visitors are not allowed to go past this point, except dead ones," the marine captain snapped as he drew a beam weapon.

"They are officials, Captain," the Sargent spluttered.

On hearing this, Frank finally realized that Andromeda was now in the hands of the military. And this Marine Captain had strict instructions to kill anyone armed and posing a threat to them.

'So, only six marines?' Frank speculated. Then, *'No, this must be a test to see how weak the Space Federation was.*

He was feeling more confident now, knowing that that had to be the marine's mission.

Chapter 9

Devil in the detail

"Why are you doing this. This ship is a civilian enterprise," Frank stated, trying to mentally disrupt the marine captain's desire to kill them all. While at the same time, he furtively put his hand behind his back to grip his second weapon, with his finger searching for the firing stud.

The marine Captain stopped twenty meters away, with his beam weapon trained on Frank. And close enough for Frank to see the marine's name on his armor.

"Captain Jerade, I am Andromeda's Captain. You and your team will not be allowed to live to tell the Earth Federation of the Military's betrayal. You will be executed as soon as you return to Earth."

"Rubbish." the captain dismissively replied.

Then Frank saw Jerade's finger hovering over his firing stud. And in one fluid motion pulled his own weapon while diving sideways to the floor in front of Sargent Stewart. With a purple beam singeing

Frank's hair as the captain's discharge narrowly missed him.

Before Frank hit the floor, he fired back, aiming at the captain's gun hand. And Jerade screamed as his hand and weapon vaporized in a purple beam.

Sargent Stewart did nothing to help his Captain. He just looked on as Jerade, still standing but in severe pain, struggled to draw another beam weapon with his remaining hand.

"Kill him," Jerade growled at Stewart, but he ignored him.

Then Frank, still on the floor, ordered Jerade to drop his weapon. But the Captain, with his beam weapon now firmly in his hand, swung around to face Frank, who instantly fired his own beam weapon, hitting the captain in the chest.

A look of horror briefly crossed Jerard's face as his body armor melted, and a light shone through a cauterized hole in his chest. Then, his body was partly vaporized in a cloud of red mist that blew out behind him. And the remains of the captain slumped to the floor, dead.

Then Frank got up from the floor and faced Sargent Stewart.

"You're not going to do anything stupid, are you?" He threateningly asked.

"No, Captain. I thought this mission was illegal to start with."

Frank looked hard at Stewart for a while as he mulled things over in his mind. And finally decided that this episode had proved a contingent of marines was needed onboard Andromeda.

Then, looking again at the Sargent, realized there was something about him, and he might just be one of the people he needed. After all, he had already proved his dedication and loyalty.

"Sargent, come with us on Andromeda's first mission as Captain of our space marines," Frank proposed.

Stewart was taken aback by the generosity of the offer.

"I appreciate your offer, Sir. But I am in the Military."

"We can easily sort that."

Stewart thought for a while, then nodded. "Then yes, Sir. Umm, how many marines have we got?" He then asked.

"At this moment in time, one," Frank replied.

"Me, I assume."

"Yes, but we'll need a contingent of six. What about the other four in your squad?" Frank asked.

Stewart thought about it. "Marcus, yes. He's in comms right now. But the remaining marines, Bryant, Hicks. And Justin, the pilot, who's still on our ship. No. They're hard nuts and too risky."

"Then you and Marcus, to start with," Frank agreed.

"So, how did you get from your ship to Andromeda?" Frank then asked Stewart.

"By Force craft via the loading bay."

"Okay, tell Marcus to stay put. Then get the other two Marines here," Frank ordered.

Stewart called Marcus and, after a short discussion, closed the contact, and a smile finally beamed across his face. Then he called Bryant and Hicks.

"Bryant, Hicks. We have new orders. Join me at the forward airlock. Now!"

"Well done, Captain," Frank acknowledged.

Stewart smiled warmly at Frank's reference to what appeared to be his promotion.

Moments later, Bryant and Hicks joined them. Both were surprised to see Frank and Stewart covering them with drawn weapons. And what appeared to be the remains of their captain, lying dead on the floor.

"Sargent, what the hell gives here?" Bryant yelled in anger.

Stewart simply looked at him with disdain.

"Both of you, place your blasters on the floor, butts first. Now," Stewart forcefully ordered.

They started to obey, but Hicks's building anger caused his hand to twitch as he began to lower his weapon to the floor.

"Don't even think about it," Frank snapped at him, bringing his beam weapon up, ready to fire.

Then Bryant and Hicks' temptation to act quickly evaporated, so they placed their weapons on the floor.

"You are both being sent back to your ship to wait for further orders," Stewart directed.

Now resigned to returning, Bryant simply muttered, "You are a double-crossing bastard." While Hicks just looked deflated and stayed silent.

Just then, Johnny's voice came through Frank's earpiece.

"Captain. Albury and the tug have already started their approach to the docking bay. So, we must hit that ship soon, or Albury will be in the way."

"Understood."

Frank and Stewart quickly escorted the two marines to the holding bay and through the holding bay's double airlock doors. Then the marines mounted their Force craft and activated its protective force field.

Once all the airlocks had closed, the air was extracted, compressed, and saved into a large recycler. The outer bay door opened, the force-craft lifted, then headed out and back to the military ship.

Meanwhile, Frank stopped the bay door from closing completely to see the force-craft entering its mother ship half a kilometer away. When it was safely inside, he partially closed the door. Counted to thirty, then called Johnny.

"Jungle Beat," Frank ordered.

"What are you doing, Captain?" Stewart asked, wondering about Frank's weird *'jungle beat'* order and why they were still here.

Then Reliant fired the particle beam weapon at its target, with devastating results.

A purple beam momentary flooded Andromeda's loading bay with an eerie light as it flashed by, just meters away.

Then the beam hit the military ship in the same area where Albury had been shot. The area flared. Glowed for a second. Then sparked before collapsing inward as the giga-joule beam dispersed.

"She's disabled, Frank," Johnny confirmed.

"Good. You'd better get the Droids to check for and repair any damage to our carrier's locking arm. And get that particle beam weapon inside Andromeda."

"Will do."

Frank turned to Stewart. "Make sure your shipmates are ok. And tell them we'll take them to Earth when we come back with the Reliant."

Stewart did as Frank instructed, pleased that Bryant, Hicks, and the pilot. would all be safe.

Frank thought about closing the holding bay door. But seeing Albury's hull closing in on them made him want to see Andromeda's critical components being unloaded.

Then he saw another small Force-craft leave the loading bay. But let it go, knowing it would be Jack and Mertoff going to the Mars spacedock.

More importantly...., there was something.... Something he couldn't quite fathom.... But that something was tugging at his mind.

Chapter 10

Andromeda

Albury bumped softly against Andromeda's hull, then her cargo doors opened.

Frank watched as several droids began transferring three large containers from Reliant into Andromeda's loading bay. Once the transfer was complete, the cargo bay door closed. Then the sling-transporter moved slowly away from Andromeda's side. Just as Frank's comm bleeped.

"Nice work Frank. Mert and I are going to the systems analysis and planning department on the Mars spacedocks right now. We're taking a force craft, and we'll pick up your two Marines on our way back to the Reliant. I reckon we'll be gone for about two hours. So, it would be a good idea for you to look around Andromeda and get the feel of her while we're gone. There are plenty of schematics located around the ship, Frank," Jack said.

"We'd like Reliant to be ready to depart for Earth at 16 hundred hours, Captain," Mert added.

Frank smiled at hearing that. "I wondered what you were up to. No problem, Reliant will be ready, and we've already ordered the sling carrier. So, Jack, have you earmarked any space in Andromeda for a small Marine contingent?"

"Not yet, Frank. But after this try-on, you should look at housing what I suppose will be our first six space marines."

"Agreed. I've already made Sargent Stewart the Captain. So, we already have two marines, counting Marcus."

There was a slight pause before Medcalf answered. "Okay, we'll go along with that. I'll get our internal design projects department to set up designated quarters, ready for when you know where you need them," Jack confirmed.

"Thanks, Jack. See you back on Reliant."

Frank checked that the bay door had closed, and re-pressurization was taking place. Then, with nothing else to do, he turned to Stewart, waiting patiently for his orders.

"I suppose you've already had a look around Andromeda?"

"Yes, Captain."

"Well. before I wander off to have a look, we need to find the best location for your Marine's quarters," Frank said. "Are there any schematics here?"

"Yes, Captain," Stewart said, pointing to a working display.

Both studied the screen that was showing Andromeda's schematics in detail. Then they started tapping on locations of interest, virtually dropping into cabins and other areas, then swinging the views around in real-time.

"These two large cabins would be ideal for the Marines. Easy access to most areas and protection for the warp drive," Frank ventured.

"Agreed. I'll check what we need to provide for our marines, Captain."

With that, Frank walked off on his own. With just under two hours to kill, he needed to spend the time well.

Frank knew from the schematics that the two short corridors leading from the central one linked the ship's technical departments and habitation section. Including Quantum Engineering, Weapons, Astro, and Data Analysis. Together with a Medical Department and other services crucial to the vessel's operation.

Frank also knew that Andromeda had several service droids that tended to the ship's physical maintenance, plus three medical droids.

The medical droids were more sophisticated and were based in the Operating Theatre, which had state-of-the-art surgical tools, and Andromeda's memory bank's resources, at their disposal. While Andromeda's processing unit, her brain, was protected deep within the ship.

But Frank was disappointed. He'd been told to wait until the proving trials on Andromeda's 'High-Brain' had been completed before seeing her. Even though he knew Andromeda's systems were fully operational.

When that was done. And the integration was complete, Andromeda would start her acceptance trials.

Frank also noted that, even though most cabins still had work to be done, he could visualize how each would eventually look. Then, remembered he had made a note to update Jack on the location they had decided on for the marines.

While he walked along, he decided it was strange that the sting on the back of his neck was still itchy, even though he couldn't feel a bump.

By the time Frank arrived at the airlock area, Captain Jerade's body was nowhere to be seen. He went on and soon located the bridge. It was just an odd-looking room that was sparsely fitted with a few familiar items and some that were new to him.

However, there was quite a bit of activity in the science labs off the far side corridor. So, Frank headed there next.

Frank was pleased that most sections had their departmental names beside their entrance doors.

And there were three extra-large workrooms for Quantum engineering, Astro, and Weapons.

Further down the corridor was another large room that seemed isolated from everything else and was off-limits. Nevertheless, Frank looked through a small window and saw several droids working on an intricate and misty-looking object that he felt sure was Andromeda's brain.

Both Astro and Weapons were still being kitted out, but no humans were present, only droids assembling equipment. The weapons department head's name, Mark Trask, already appeared under the section name, as did Tim Watson's, under Astro.

Quantum engineering was the exception. It appeared to be operational, and Ned Parker's name showed under the section name.

Frank opened the door and approached a burly man sitting at one of four massive consoles with virtual displays, input arrays, and simulators.

"Hello, Ned Parker, is it?" Frank asked as he reached the man.

The white-haired man dressed in a gray work suit looked up.

"What do you want?" He snapped at Frank.

Taken aback by the man's attitude, Frank unsmilingly continued.

"Just being friendly."

"Well, bugger-off. Can't you see I'm busy?"

"I suppose I'll have to call you Grumpy from now on," Frank replied as he turned to leave.

"Who the hell are you anyway?"

"Andromeda's Captain," Frank answered and went back into the corridor. He felt sure that Ned Parker's eyes were following him out.

Well, that was uncomfortable, Frank thought. *Ned's attitude is unacceptable onboard my ship.*

Frank was pleased after what seemed ages when Johnny's long-awaited call finally came through.

"Frank, directors Medcalf, Mertoff, and the two marines, Marcus and Stewart, are all back on the Reliant."

"What about the three marines on the military ship?"

"Stewart told them he's now in charge of the marines and has tried to persuade them to join us. But they insist that another ship will pick them up."

"They'll have a long wait," Frank pointed out. Then, as an afterthought, he contacted Jack.

"Jack, you should instruct Mars central to still view that military ship and its rescuer as hostile. And, to cover them with a weapon's platform or something."

"Good thinking, Frank. I'll do it now."

Then Frank headed back to the Reliant via the transfer tube.

One hour later, and well outside the Mars exclusion zone, the fast Carrier vessel arrived and started maneuvering into position to enable the Reliant to lock on.

The automatic docking commenced as the two vessels moved closer. Then Reliant's curved, claw-like locking arm contacted the Carrier's locking mechanism. A slight jarring bump, and the two vessels were locked together.

"Locked," Johnny confirmed. "Countdown, one minute."

The countdown finally reached zero, and the Group jerked forward as the Carrier's massive drive engines went to full power.

The two-hour return trip to Earth had finally commenced.

Chapter 11

Back to Earth

Once the initial acceleration diminished, Marcus and Stewart left the Reliant's flight deck with Director Mertoff to discuss their requirements. While Jack joined Frank and Johnny on the flight deck.

"Do you want me to leave you two alone, Frank?" Johnny asked, sensing they wanted to discuss something privately.

"No need," Frank replied. "Uh, is that ok, Jack?"

"It's up to you. Nothing top secret, I assure you," Jack said, smiling.

"Okay, Jack. Shoot."

"As I said, you can live with Georgina and me until Andromeda's ready to start her proving trials. That'll be in about four months. This will give you time to train on SpaceFed's flight simulators, then have the Transceiver inserted.

Remember, the insert must be fully integrated with your brain and working perfectly before Andromeda's Hyper brain comes online in early January."

"Well, that gives me just two months... OK." Frank said and thought about it for a while.

"So, I won't be joining her until her proving trials start, is that right?"

"Correct," Jack confirmed.

"Am I the only one with this experimental Transceiver?" Frank then asked.

"No, the rest of the crew already have simplified versions, as will your new marines."

"Even so, can I assume I'm the real Guineapig?" Frank asked.

"In a way. But your Transceiver will also have millions of neurons and synaptic-mimicking connections. However, even that won't be sufficient, don't worry. The cell filaments will eventually bond, and you will be one with Andromeda."

"Okay. So, what's the timeline for Andromeda to be ready for a flight?" Frank then asked Jack.

"Thanks to you, Andromeda's High-brain can still be activated in early January. Then, the proving and acceptance testing will be completed in March, with you on board," Jack explained.

"And her first mission should start just a couple of weeks after that," he added. Then Mert came back.

"You know I'll be 37 on January the 6th, don't you?" Frank asked them both.

"Yes. Then you'll start your 37th with a bang," Mert joked.

"Christ. I hope not."

The chit-chat continued over the next two hours, with Frank and Jack bonding well. Then they were interrupted by the carrier vessel's flight control, notifying them that just ten minutes remained until they reached Earth.

Ten minutes later, the Reliant and its Carrier vessel halted, 420 kilometers out from Earth.

"Welcome back, Captain Richardson," came Earth's space operations controller. "A shuttle with your relief team on board will be with you in fifteen minutes."

"Thanks. We'll be glad for some rest," Frank replied.

"I'm sure. The carrier vessel will remain locked with Reliant. in readiness for a service checkup on the locking arm."

"Understood," Frank acknowledged. Then, turning to the others onboard, suggested, "We'd better get ready to leave."

Then Frank and Johnny set their shut-down sequence to standby mode in readiness for the coming change-over.

Once satisfied, they collected their personal things, then joined the others in the passenger area. Just as Mertoff's pad received an update from Earth's Space Federation's movement director.

"Listen up, everyone. After reading the content, we have an update that makes sense," Mertoff remarked.

"Yes, and…?" Frank impatiently queried.

"Stewart and Marcus will come with me for debriefing and induction into Andromeda's crew."

"Anything else?"

Mertoff couldn't help smiling at Jack. "Frank, you'll be seeing the lovely Georgina very soon. And as for you, Johnny, your month's break is still on."

"Thank goodness," Johnny declared.

"So, all's tickety-boo then," Jack jokingly put in.

"Nobody uses that phrase anymore, Jack. Too old fashioned," an annoyed Mertoff pointed out.

"Bah. You should lighten up, Mert."

"Time to move," Frank instructed, ignoring their chit-chat.

Then, deep in their thoughts, they all moved off to the main airlock to transfer to the Earth shuttle. Which was on its final approach and visible on the lock's side display.

Moments later, the external force-field transfer tube was established.

Once the greenish-colored *'Airtight'* light illuminated, the Reliant's airlock doors opened. Then three men, a woman, and their large service container drifted through the shuttle's shimmering transfer tube into Reliant's open airlock.

All four acknowledged Jack and Mertoff on seeing the Starship and Star emblems on their uniforms as they entered. Then both groups shook hands as the newcomers exited the tube and boarded Reliant.

"Hello, Frank, I hear you've had quite a trip, according to our updates," Captain Andrews said, greeting him.

"Hi, Ted. Yes, it was a bit hairy, to say the least. But thankfully, Johnny and the Droid managed to straighten the locking claw arm enough to get us back."

"Our techs will sort the claw out, Frank."

"Thanks. We've left the ship in standby mode," Frank added.

"Excellent."

"Come on. Let's stop all this chattering," Mertoff impatiently said. "We've got urgent things to do on Earth."

Then, all six made their way to the waiting shuttle and onward to Earth.

Chapter 12

Georgina

Frank took the induction-powered monorail from the Spaceport out to his old apartment in Hampstead to collect his belongings. Then, the monorail straight on to Knightsbridge.

Frank used the multi-track moving walkway that formed part of the sidewalk to reach Jack and Georgina's luxurious apartment in Knightsbridge. This area was north of the Thames River and still one of the most expensive in the U.K.

The front door slid open as he approached. And an attractive woman, dressed in a long dark red garment, stepped into view and beckoned him in.

"Georgina?" he queried as he stepped inside the massive, plush entrance hall.

"Yes. Hello, Frank," she replied, tilting her head.

Frank took the hint and kissed her on her cheek, then stepped back.

"I feel I already know you, from all the good things Jack has been bending my ear with," she added, seeing Frank's hesitancy.

Frank knew that Georgina was in her late forties and considerably younger than Jack. And had an air of aloofness about her. Even so, she reminded him of his mother.

He couldn't help staring at Georgina while noting her tanned look, almost black eyes, and dark brown hair. *'Colombian, for sure,'* he thought.

"I was born in Colombia," she said, anticipating his next question.

"You must be a mind reader," Frank jokingly replied.

"No. Everyone asks me that same question. You know the most beautiful women come from there, don't you?"

"Well, I do now."

Georgina turned to face a security panel next to the door and looked directly at its sensor lens. Waited a moment while it scanned her iris. Then, a small virtual screen formed from an unseen projector on one side of the panel. Georgina tapped in her security code, then turned and said, "Now you, Frank. Please."

Knowing what was expected of him, Frank tapped in his national security code and waited for his iris scan to complete.

"Now, push your right thumb slowly through the virtual screen," Georgina ordered.

His thumb tingled as it passed through. Then the virtual screen vanished.

"All done, Frank," Georgina stated. "You can come and go as you please."

"This is kind of you both to put me up like this."

"Jack seems to like you," she said, smiling. "So, we'd better get you settled in before he finishes his work. Follow me," she said and headed for the second door on the left.

"I've put you in here, Frank. It's close to the front door, so you won't disturb us with whatever you need to do."

"Thank you, Georgina," he said as the door silently slid open and revealed a small but well-equipped, self-contained apartment.

"You can call me Georgie," she said. "Come straight through to the lounge when you've freshened up."

"Thanks."

With that, she left him to settle in.

Frank unpacked his belongings and checked out the apartment. The only thing that surprised him was the food synthesizer. It was far more sophisticated than the one on the Mars transporter. But, by its side, Georgina had left a list of special food and drinks that weren't generally in a synthesizer's memory.

Twenty minutes later, Frank ambled into the Medcalf's spacious lounge.

Still dressed in her dark red garment, Georgina sat on a curved, pale blue sofa. She glanced at him, smiled, and then pointed to the seat next to her.

"Glad you made it, my boy," Jack greeted as he took Frank a whiskey on the rocks from the vending machine.

"How did you know I like whiskey that way?"

"I make it a habit to know about people I might have to deal with," Jack stated as Frank took the drink and sat down next to Georgina.

"You'll find him very nosey. And annoying at times," she remarked as Jack sat on the other side.

"Then I'll have to get used to Jack," Frank jokingly replied while casting his eye around the room.

His eyes locked onto a large picture sitting on a modern cabinet. The smartly clad woman in the picture seemed to be calling him.

"Is she a family member?" Frank asked Jack

"Yes. It is my….

"She was staying with us while completing her training," Georgina said, sharply interrupting Jack.

"May I take a look at her picture?"

Both Jack and Georgina looked at each other before answering.

"Yes. But be careful with it," Georgina warned.

"It'll turn into a Holo image when you pick it up," Jack added.

Frank sensed their reluctance for him to look at the woman in the picture, which intrigued him even more.

So, he put his glass of whiskey down on a tray that seemed to have come from nowhere. Then, stood to pick up the picture but suddenly stopped.

It was then that Frank felt a mental change in himself. He was sure his thought processing had moved up a gear, and his cognitive thoughts were clear and sharper.

"Are you alright, Frank," Georgina asked, somewhat concerned at seeing him stop and look blank for a moment.

"Yes... Just a strange feeling," Frank replied. Then felt for the bump on the back of his neck. But it wasn't there anymore. Just an itchy patch.

'Was this all to do with that buzzing sound? And the minus two-minute time discrepancy between Earth's time-sync transmitter and my transporter's time clock?' He wondered.

This made Frank sweat again, but he picked up the photo anyway. Then almost dropped the picture as a Holo image of the woman's upper body suddenly expanded out of the picture. And he found himself staring into the woman's blue-green eyes.

This stunned Frank for a moment.

"How old was she when this was taken?" Frank finally managed to ask.

"It was taken five years ago, when she was 29," Georgina reluctantly answered.

"So, she would be 34 now?"

"That would be correct," Jack agreed.

"Have I met her before, Jack?"

"Not that I'm aware of."

"She is certainly beautiful," Frank said as he slowly rotated the Holo image before putting the picture back on the cabinet.

Frank sat down again. Took up his glass and sipped the drink slowly as he thought about the picture while savoring every drop.

"Is this no-name woman likely to come here soon?"

"She would not want us to talk about her, Frank," Georgina stated. "And no, she will not be returning soon."

"Let's get something to eat, Georgie," Jack urged, changing the subject. "It's been a long day."

"An excellent idea, Jack," she agreed. "Frank will be able to try out some of the special dishes in Andromeda's new food replicator."

"Ah, I thought the synthesizer was a bit over the top for a home," Frank stated as they got up and moved to the dining area.

Frank sat waiting, wondering why Georgina had said to him, '*with whatever you need to do.*'

Then Jack whispered in his ear. "Georgina gave her word not to talk about the no-name woman to you. So, don't bring it up again; there's a good fellow."

"Of course not, Jack," Frank agreed but wondered why the embargo.

"Nevertheless, you will see her in the future," Jack quietly added.

But why doesn't the no-name woman want Georgina to talk to me about her, he wondered.

It must be something I've missed. But what?

Chapter 13

Ghost

Frank was ordered to attend an induction course, at the SpaceFed Intelligence Unit, for a complete mental and physical assessment. The unit was close to Reading and the old Microsoft Campus.

The following five days were hectic for him, with many physical and mental tests. Then new documentation was collated, including information about his overall fitness, retina scans, and DNA.

Frank also spent time with the developers of the Transceiver at Dacta Micros. To learn how it would meld with the cerebrum's corpus callosum nerves in his brain to enable it to interface with the transceiver.

Frank struggled to understand how the tiny Implant's *filaments* had decided where they would bond. What a microRNA coding error meant for him. And what synaptic vesicles, or something like that, did.

Now, Frank accepted that he had left *Dacta Micros* with at least a reasonable understanding of what he was letting himself in for.

During the following week, Frank attended an intense awareness program to understand how Andromeda worked. And to familiarize him with the ship.

The use of flight and layout simulators gave Frank a frighteningly realistic operational feel for Andromeda. This, in turn, gave him confidence in knowing how to tackle any awkward and dangerous situations they might encounter.

Luckily, his training with *Warbend Elite*, and his recent encounter with the military, had also given him a head start.

After which, Captaincy of Andromeda data was obtained and filed with SpaceFed security before her High-Brain was activated. This data would also be embedded in Andromeda's security block.

Then the day finally came for Frank to have his new Transceiver fitted at Dacta Micros. He entered the specialist surgical development Lab Eleven and was prepped and anesthetized for this complicated and dangerous procedure.

Although the operation was successful. Frank had to spend the next three days in a rigid support frame. While continuing his education on the transceiver by watching several training sequences run by a Miss

Chaple. These included thought generation, sight, speech, and hearing sampling. This was necessary to allow the Implant's multiplying filaments to start bonding with the relevant active areas in his brain's cerebrum corpus callosum nerve fibers.

"Remember, Frank, you must keep up the medication, or you'll feel like your brain is being eaten," the surgeon had warned him.

And he wasn't wrong, Frank thought. Feeling like he had to scratch his head. Or better still, dig out his flesh and rip the implant out.

He'd been ordered not to do any physical work for another week. After that, he would have an implant progress examination at Lab Eleven to determine if the merger between his brain and the implant was progressing satisfactorily before he could work again. But Frank ignored that order and, on the 4th of December, went back to Jack Medcalf's residence.

He arrived at three-thirty, but no one was in. So, Frank went straight to his apartment. Sorted out the clothes that needed cleaning and put them into the sterilizing and refresher unit. Then packed the rest away.

Then Frank took his medication and dialed a snack from the food replicator. Frank felt very tired by now, so he selected a holo-movie from the entertainment center. Then sat back on his sofa and relaxed as the holographic movie started…; then fell fast asleep.

Frank woke with a start to find the movie running. He still felt dozy and thought he saw someone silhouetted in the open doorway. But by the time he had got himself together, the person had gone.

"Damn," he muttered as he stood up and checked the entrance hall. But the hall was empty.

Then, he quickly checked everything in his apartment, but nothing was missing as far as he could tell.

Just then, Jack and Georgina came back.

"Hello, Frank," Georgina greeted him as she saw him standing in his doorway. "Did the operation go well?" She asked.

"Yes. Though it was a much bigger deal than I expected. I feel exhausted, Georgie."

"It'll pass, Frank," Jack remarked on his way to the lounge. "Come and join us when you're ready."

"Give me a couple of minutes," Frank said. As Georgina followed Jack into the lounge and dialed up a drink and snack.

Frank joined them ten minutes later.

"If it's a whiskey you need, there's a sub-menu for zero alcohol drinks," Jack pointed out without looking up from his work pad.

"Thanks."

As Frank collected his alcohol-free drink, Georgina pointed to a firmer-looking seat facing them. He nodded and sat down.

Once seated, he went to speak, but Jack put a hand up in dismissal. Frank took the hint and sipped his drink while noticing that the 'no-name' female's photo had disappeared from the cabinet.

A short time later, Jack looked up from his work pad.

"So, what will you do until Andromeda's ready to start her acceptance trials?"

"Well, I've got plenty of mandatory checks and training sessions at Lab Eleven, which will fill some of the time."

"Don't overdo it," Georgina warned.

"I'll be careful. Nevertheless, I need to find something more challenging to do than just sitting around the rest of the time," Frank replied.

Then added, "Andromeda's Hyper brain isn't due to come online until January."

"So what?" Jack replied.

"I'll be 37 by then!" Frank exclaimed.

That's no age. I'm still working, and I'll be 56 soon," Jack stated.

"I think 2301 will be a nerve-wracking year," Jack added after a few minutes while wondering if they had seen the last of Winton's military endeavors.

"I see your no-name lodger's photo has gone," Frank said, pointing at the cabinet.

"She came in yesterday and took it away," Georgina stated.

"That's strange. I'm sure she was here earlier. Or maybe it was a ghost standing in my doorway," Frank suggested.

"Rubbish. Anyway, you'll see her next year," Jack firmly stated.

"Okay, but you've both known me long enough by now... I haven't been with anyone since Paula. So, what's the big deal with me showing an interest and wanting to see her?"

"You just need to abide by her wishes, Frank," Georgina added, sounding stressed.

"Sorry, Georgie. I'll keep off the subject."

"About time," Jack said and turned his attention to his work pad.

Then Frank noted that Georgina had relaxed. And knew his stay with them would be the tonic he needed.

Over the intervening days, Frank recovered fully and worked with Jack on various Andromeda-related problems. He also attended several training sessions and meetings with Mertoff and Dacta Micros.

Then Christmas and the New year came and went with minimal celebrations. And, to Frank's disappointment, the no-name girl in the picture never came back.

Chapter 14

The Briefing

January 19th

Two days after Frank's thirty-seventh birthday, he was summoned to Space Federation's U.K. complex for the final briefing before joining Andromeda.

He was greeted by a 22cm diameter, saucer-shaped drone floating close to the main entrance.

"Follow me, sir," it requested and headed inside the building.

Frank managed to keep pace with the drone as it flew across the foyer, along several linking corridors, and finally into a large room with people sitting around a circular table.

The drone then hovered over an empty seat. Frank took the hint and sat down while quickly taking note of the other five people around the table. There were two women and three men.

All five eyed him as he sat down, and Frank acknowledged them with a nod.

He already knew Jack Medcalf and Mertoff. But the other three were unknown to him. The man in the center with an oversized electronic pad was undoubtedly a higher rank than Jack or Mertoff. Maybe he was from intelligence, Frank speculated.

"Welcome, Captain," the smartly dressed, almost white-haired man in the center greeted him. "I am Commissioner James Carter."

"Good morning, sir," Frank courteously replied.

"I understand you already know Directors Medcalf and Mertoff," Carter stated.

"Yes, sir."

"So let me introduce Alina Smirnov, the head of Astro Tracking."

"Nice to meet you, Alina," Frank acknowledged, looking directly at the expressionless middle-aged blonde woman.

"And you, Captain," she replied.

"Lastly, Jesica Chaple from Dacta Micros," Carter finished.

"Ah. I thought I recognized you, Jesica," Frank exclaimed. Remembering this thirty-something dark-haired and extremely attractive woman as the person who had helped him during his three-day transceiver training at Dactos.

"I'm surprised you remember me, Captain," she said, blushing slightly.

"Not at all. If I wasn't disappearing for a few months or even years, I'd certainly think about asking you out."

Jesica smiled at Frank but didn't respond to his flattery.

"Well, let's get down to business…. Let's start with you, Jack," the Commissioner urged.

"Alright. Both Mert and I have been keeping Frank up to date. So, there isn't much we can add," Jack simply replied.

"Agreed. Unfortunately, your Marines will not be on the proving trials with you, Frank. A technical security issue has been raised by Command," Mert chipped in.

This surprised Frank. "I would have thought the marines were necessary, going by the Navy's past action with Andromeda," he said, stating the obvious.

"We all agree with you, Frank. But Command doesn't know the marines from Adam. And more importantly, all the marines have come from the Navy. So, Command will not take the risk. We must honor their orders," Jack pointed out.

"I'm afraid there's no way around it, Frank," Commissioner Carter agreed.

"So…, Alina?" Carter prompted.

Alina Smirnov's *work-pad* glowed, and a Holo projection hovered above the table about a meter in diameter.

This display showed a four-light-year spherical area of Space, with Hawk's expected flight path and final location showing as a yellow line of light.

"This is as close as we can get in predicting where the Hawk is most likely to be," she said.

"That's a big area to search," Frank commented.

"Agreed. And it's complicated. With too many variables," Alina told him, then continued.

"The Galaxy is moving in one direction, but most of its stars are moving at different velocities. For instance, Sol's position, related to Procyon's, is not only at a different point in space than they were five years ago. But the gravimetric distortion of both stars could cause space-time to warp, and curve or bend your wormhole."

"But we must have the technology to get closer to the point where Hawk should be, shouldn't we?" Frank asked, interrupting Alina.

"A whole department is dedicated to doing just that, Frank. By the time Andromeda is due to leave on her mission, you'll get the latest predicted trajectory and location via a finger-print Security Capsule," Alina explained.

"Why not just transmit it directly to Andromeda?"

"We're not sure how closely Naval intelligence can monitor us, Frank," Alina replied while thinking about it.

"The man you know as *AF* will deliver the capsule personally when he boards," she added.

"That's all I can ask," he returned, thinking that the only *AF* he knew had to be Alan Fairchild. Alan had started the pilot training course but dropped out halfway through. And Frank had no idea what had happened to him since.

"Are we done, Alina?"

"I think so, Commissioner. Unless Frank has any more questions."

"No, Alina. That was quite comprehensive."

"Okay…. Jesica?"

"Our continuous monitoring of Frank's implant shows it responds as expected. So, we don't see a problem when Frank mentally turns on Andromeda's High-Brain link," Jesica confidentially stated.

"I have to admit I rarely notice the implant is even there anymore," Frank commented.

"That is as we hoped, Frank. And your crew's implants are less intrusive than yours," Jesica pointed out.

"So, you'll have to train Andromeda, and your implant, to suppress what you don't need to hear. And save what you need to hear in the implant's four Terabyte Memory.

We have no firm data on what you will experience. But we are confident you will both link, and the experience will be fantastic. Nevertheless, remember, it will be a continuous learning curve for Andromeda, which you will be a part of."

"Like teaching a child," Frank joked.

"Maybe, but a child who will surpass you in every area," Jessica firmly stated.

Frank stopped himself from coming out with any more jokes and simply asked. "So, what's next?"

"Just another addition to your link with Andromeda," Jesica said as she stood up. Then came around behind him, holding a small instrument in her hand.

"Now, Commissioner?" Jesica asked.

Commissioner James Carter looked around at everyone else for confirmation. All nodded in agreement.

"Yes, Jesica. Activate the control sequence," he ordered.

"You won't feel anything, Frank," she said as she held one end of the instrument against the area where his implant was located. The device glowed a moment, then clicked off.

"All done, Frank," she confirmed and sat down again.

"We've embedded some security codes in your implant for you to use if needed," Commissioner Carter explained. "These automatically activate Andromeda's security block. Please note that one set of codes will place Andromeda's High-Brain into sleep mode."

"Do you mean I can put Andromeda to sleep?" Frank queried.

"Yes. But only you or a Mars security technician can override the sleep command to wake her up," Mertoff interjected.

The Commissioner studied his work pad for a moment, then turned to speak to Jack.

"Jack, you can deliver the formal instructions to Frank now. Show them as said in our presence, and for the record."

"Sure, Commissioner," he acknowledged and selected the agreed text.

"Frank, you will join Andromeda as her Captain on the twenty-seventh of this month. And conduct her acceptance trials in conjunction with the civilian personnel.

It is expected that the trials will be completed by February the tenth. With Andromeda being handed over to the Space Federation by February the eighteenth.

Your first mission is to find the Hawk. You will leave by March the seventh at the latest. And you will assume complete authority for the mission." Jack said, paused, then continued…

"A full report of this meeting will shortly be sent to your new tactical pad. Including listings of the expected civilian personnel and the ship's itinerary," Jack finished.

"Are you ready to wrap this meeting up, now?" the Commissioner asked.

"Yes, we're all done," Mertoff answered for everyone. "Any queries in the meantime can be easily dealt with."

"Then the meeting is closed," Commissioner James Carter stated. Then stood up and walked around the table to Frank.

"Good Luck, Frank," he said and shook his hand.

The meeting then ended.

"Shall we go home and take it easy for the rest of the day, Frank?"

"Agreed."

Chapter 15

Double Trouble

January 27th
07:53, local time

Eight days later, Frank, dressed in his dark blue Captain's uniform, with its Starship across a star background emblem on each shoulder. Left Jack and Georgina's home early after saying his goodbyes.

He was looking forward to seeing them again on the tenth of February, assuming Andromeda's trials went well.

Frank took a high-speed *Magnetic-levitation* train to the London Spaceport Hub adjacent to Stansted Airport.

The airport had been recently expanded to handle the sizeable nuclear-powered transport aircraft that linked each continental hub.

Frank sat back in his seat as the mag-train accelerated and, within seconds, was hurtling along at over four hundred kilometers an hour. Arriving seven minutes later.

The super small auto-check-in Droid scanned Frank's retina and thumbprint. Then Frank's personal travel case opened with a slight hiss. Then auto-closed and relocked after the scan.

"You are late, sir," the droid coldly stated. "Just follow the signs to Embarkation Zone 7. Then enter the transfer transporter, which will take you to Shuttle E3."

"Well, that's told me off," Frank muttered as he hurried to the embarkation point.

The large E7 capsule-shaped and semitransparent transporter was waiting, beckoning Frank in... He boarded and sat in the closest seat.

The transporter rose a few centimeters off the ground as its entrance door closed. Then surged forward and out into the open, heading for the E3 Shuttle waiting to take Frank into orbit, where it would dock with a *Sling transporter*.

The shuttle would then take its group of passengers and cargo to Mars and Andromeda.

Before entering the Space shuttle, Frank had made sure his mag shoes were comfortable. Then he was shown to a seat by another even more diminutive Droid. He sat down and acknowledged the other four passengers close to him. But he was disappointed to see no windows in the passenger cabin.

So, the shuttle's purely a utilitarian vessel, he decided.

Within moments of Frank being secured in his seat, the shuttle's airlock closed. Then Frank felt the shuttle lift off the ground using its high-powered field emitters. Then came a groaning sound as the forward emitter's power went to Max, causing the shuttle's nose to tilt upward.

Then, her twin Beckner pulse engines came to life, and Frank felt the G force increase rapidly as the shuttle rocketed forward and upward.

No one spoke during the twenty-minute flight to the Sling transporter.

Frank was pleasantly surprised to see that the waiting Sling vessel was his old ship, Reliant. And as the group of four passengers boarded, a voice called out to him from the flight deck.

"Welcome aboard, Frank," Captain Andrews greeted him.

"Good to see you again, Ted."

"And you. Bring your things and sit with us."

"Okay."

Frank entered the flight deck, shook hands with Ted, and placed his personal travel case next to one of the two spare anti-inertia seats at the back of the flight deck.

"This is Jason," Ted said, pointing to his co-pilot cum dog's body.

"Nice to meet you, Sir," Jason said as they shook hands.

"Heard a lot about you, Sir," Jason added as he acknowledged the Earth shuttle's confirmation of its separation from Reliant'.

"Shuttle clear in one minute," Jason notified his Captain.

"Good...That dull-looking metal container in the corner was left for you by a Jack Medcalf," the captain told Frank. "It's unscannable," he added.

Frank looked at it and wondered how Jack had managed to get this large rectangular-shaped container onboard. 'Come to that, should he look inside just in case its contents were important?' He hesitated, then decided to leave it until they got to Mars, and he was on his own.

"Thanks, Ted. I'll remember to take it when we get to Mars."

"Right. Move to the Carrier arrester point on the mark," the captain ordered. As he entered the expected lock-on point and time into the Carrier net.

"Check on our other passengers," he then ordered Jason.

Jason left the flight deck to check the other four passengers were settled in and secure. And was back within two minutes and sitting in the engineer's seat.

"All four secure. Some are snoozing, some reading," Jason reported. Then carried out his final system checks.

Then he set the auto-sequence to join and attach Reliant to the waiting crewless *fast carrier* vessel C5. This vessel would take them straight to Mars and Andromeda.

"Set to go, Captain. Auto sequence synced with C5," Jason confirmed.

Frank sat quietly in his inertia-dampening seat, following the progression as the automatic system took over.

A short time later, the commencement warning light flashed. Reliant accelerated for a few seconds, then halted under the waiting Carrier.

Reliant then moved upwards to automatically dock with their carrier transporter.

"Locking arm locked and secured," Jason informed.

"One minute to transit initiation."

"Thirty seconds," Jason then warned.

The captain read the final countdown aloud so all could hear. "Five... Four... Three... Two... One... Zero."

And the C5 carrier jerked forward as its massive drive engines went to full power.

Frank sunk back into his seat. Automatically gritting his teeth while enjoying every moment, as usual.

Once the acceleration stabilized, there was little to do until they reached Mars, as the auto systems were in control.

"We should reach Mars's exclusion zone in…, two hours, five minutes," Jason notified everyone, then relaxed.

Then the captain turned to speak to Frank.

"I'll be glad when the new shuttles take over this run. Then we'll be non-stop from Earth to Mars in just four hours. That's got to be better than this, Frank," Ted ventured while clearly pondering something else.

"I reckon you're right. Is something else bothering you?" Frank then queried.

"Yeah. Tell me why so many supposedly 'inspection personnel' are needed on Andromeda?"

Frank thought through Ted's question before answering.

"How many are we talking about?"

"Well, I took the snagging and approval team to Andromeda myself. Which was about nine people in all… But Albury then took another nine. Who, in my opinion, had a questionable reason to be on Andromeda. Listen to this message, Frank," Ted urged. "It was left for you by Captain Rankin."

Then selected 'Play Rankin message. Flight-deck only.' And the message played out on the comms.

'Hello Frank, I think my last transfer of nine individuals to Andromeda is suspect… They may be military-orientated… Just be careful... Rankin. Out.'

Frank's heart sank.

Not again, he thought and looked at the dull-looking container Jack Medcalf had left for him.

"Jack must have seen this coming," he said out loud.

"What was that you said, Frank?" Ted asked.

Frank didn't reply. But his mind felt sharper than ever, and he was already playing through scenarios like never before.

Chapter 16

Frank and the Box

January 27th
20:53, Mars station, local time

The view of Mars filled Reliant's front flight-deck windows, with the B4 spacedock facilities orbiting Mars standing out in relief against Mars's red backdrop.

While Andromeda. Just fifteen kilometers further out from the docks and illuminated by six *Lummi* buoys positioned a hundred meters away, shone like a golden cigar against the stars.

The thrill of knowing that Andromeda was his to command brought a lump to Frank's throat. And seeing this golden oval-shaped Starship again, with each end tapering to a point, was more than Frank's wildest dreams could ever have imagined.

Andromeda was a kilometer long and a hundred meters in diameter at her widest point.

Frank could just make out the fixed secondary jump ring, flush-mounted in the outer hull in front of the sub-light unit. This worked in conjunction with the primary Jump ring when creating a wormhole.

Andromeda's primary warp focusing ring was situated sixty meters back from the front of the ship. Each section of this ring extended outwards virtually instantaneously, with sliding parts closing the gaps to complete a full circle some fifty meters out from the hull.

"Ten minutes before we dock at B4 station's airlock," Jason informed everyone over the ship's comms.

"Do I have to disembark there?" Frank asked.

"No, just four of the station's construction team who are returning from vacation. But you're the only one going on to Andromeda, Captain," Andrew told Frank.

"Okay. Then I think it's about time I had a quick look in Jack's box."

"Hit the blue tab to your left," Ted suggested. Frank did so, and a rectangular platform rose from the flight deck floor.

"Great," he exclaimed and lifted Jack's large but surprisingly light box onto it. Under the lower gravity of the Reliant, the box weighed a third of its actual weight.

Frank checked the box and saw it was a seamless container with no visible locks or hinges. In fact, there wasn't even any sign of an opening.

Then he noticed a thumbprint scanner's rectangular pad on the front. Placed his thumb on its sensor, and the top part of the box dissolved, exposing the contents in seconds. Frank saw the micro field emitters that created its lid, or barrier, just inside the box. But there was no sign of a power source in this open section.

Further down, amongst a mass of items, were eight compact hand-held beam weapons that were smaller than any Frank had used before. He sighed with relief at the welcome sight.

Just then, the captain turned and looked towards the box. "Geeze, Frank. Are you kitting an army?" he asked, seeing several of the hand weapons on view.

"No," Frank replied. "But I reckon someone thinks I need to."

"Docking in one-minute thirty," Jason announced as *Reliant* moved closer to the B4 station's airlock.

"You'd better decide what you're going to do before we dock with Andromeda, Frank. That'll be in… twenty-one minutes," Ted warned.

"Okay, will do. Don't worry," Frank assured him.

Reliant's transfer tube was then established with B4's airlock receptors. Then the four construction personnel swiftly transferred into the Space dock's main tech and habitation facility.

Once the transfer had been completed, Reliant separated and headed out to Andromeda, just fifteen kilometers from the Docks.

In the meantime, Frank had selected two of the eight hand weapons in the box. Placed one in his side pocket and tucked the other in the back of his uniform. Then put his thumb on the thumbprint scanner's pad, and the container's lid reformed, sealing the box.

"We're passing the one-minute marker, Captain," Jason informed him as Reliant closed in on Andromeda's main airlock.

Frank acknowledged this. Got up and shook hands with Captain Andrews and Jason. Then picked up his case and Jack's container.

"Remember *Rankin's* warning, Frank. Just be careful," Ted reiterated as Frank went off to Reliant's airlock

"I will."

A minute later, Reliant's field emitters created the transfer tube with Andromeda. Once the tube's integrity had been confirmed, the air pressure had equalized, and their lock-status lights had changed to green. Reliant and Andromeda's airlock doors then opened.

Frank stepped inside the shimmering transfer tube and, with a gentle push, drifted across to

Andromeda's open airlock. Then into her reception area.

Before Frank's feet touched the floor, Andromeda's inner and outer airlock doors closed.

Frank knew Reliant would now collapse the transfer tube. Close her airlock and prepare to back away from Andromeda before heading off on the Sling ship's transport duty.

Frank also knew there wouldn't be any Cavalry charging over some mystical hill to bail him out.

From here on, he was on his own.

Frank placed his luggage on the floor, checked the time on his wrist pad, and saw it had changed to Ship-time and was now reading 06:00 hours. Then checked who was near him and saw several men just standing around the central corridor junction, seemingly with nothing to do.

Then a tall slim man, with a jerky-looking walk, hurried up the corridor towards him.

"Captain Richardson?" the man asked as he came to a halt in front of Frank.

"Yes?"

"Welcome aboard. I'm Andrew Carden, the approvals coordinator."

"Nice to meet you, Andrew," Frank said, acknowledging this pleasant-sounding man. Then looking him over, decided his almost disheveled look didn't seem out of place.

"I guess you're a scientist," Frank added.

127

"Yes, Quantum physics, Captain."

"Call me Frank. So, that means you'll have met grumpy old Ned Parker?"

Andrew smiled. "Yes. But we get along... He's quite clever, and with it."

"That's all we can ask for, especially on this trip."

Andrew then handed him a small device. "These communicators will enable us to talk to each other without using Andromeda's comms system."

"That makes sense," Frank said as he looked it over.

"Right. I know it's your ship, Frank. But time is short, and we've been instructed to complete the trials as soon as possible. Everything seems to be working correctly on the ship, but we may have to make some tweaks during testing," Andrew told Frank, then paused briefly.

"Understood," Frank stated. "Although I don't share the Federation's hope that there are any survivors on the Hawk."

"Me neither," Andrew agreed.

"You obviously know your way around Andromeda, Frank. So, join us in the recreation suite after you've freshened up. A meeting to set the protocols has been scheduled there. And, I believe, for you to activate Andromeda's *High-Mind*.... Let's say...in one hour, okay?"

"Fine. But Andromeda can function without her human side, anyway," Frank replied with a smile.

"That is true... However, I'm worried about a group of nine personnel that arrived earlier from the Albury. I'm not sure what they are here for. But they are pushing to fully activate Andromeda earlier than the acceptance trial's schedule stipulates."

"I see. I'll check them before the meeting commences, Andrew," Frank assured him.

"Thanks. I'll see you later," Andrew replied as he turned and jerkily headed back up the corridor.

I bet the nine layabouts are the same ones Ted warned me about. Frank decided as he picked up his belongings and walked off to the captain's cabin, in the same jerky fashion as Andrew had, with his mag boots dragging along the mosaic floor.

Then Frank checked the weapons locker outside his cabin and found it empty. This concerned him, especially if someone knew that the nine were military.

Chapter 17

Mind Bender

Andromeda's AI, using a minute part of her processing capability, carried out the tasks needed to run the ship to the letter of her programmed directive. While controlling everything on board the vessel.

But there was no emotion or humanity about Andromeda's actions. There was a void in her memory banks Andromeda realized. Something was missing. Something that would change her forever.

Perhaps another advanced AI would merge with her and make her feel complete, Andromeda speculated.

She felt that whatever it was, it was close to happening. But how could it? When there only seemed to be humans on board, with no other AI's listed as joining her.

Frank unpacked and stowed his belongings in the cabin adjacent to Andromeda's control room. He knew the layout well from his numerous sessions in the flight simulator on Earth. Then he hid Jack's container out of sight and went back to the control room.

"Supply a comfortable chair and a small table," Frank ordered aloud, unsure if all audio commanded systems were operational. But it certainly looked like it as the control room's virtual systems powered up.

Thankfully, Andrew was right, and an object rose out of the floor, morphing into a comfortable chair as it went. Then, another thing rose, configuring itself into an occasional table, and was placed next to the chair. Frank knew additional facilities would also rise from the floor and auto-configure when needed.

He sat down for a moment to take in the current situation. He knew he needed to modify his actions to confuse any takeover attempt, especially when acting differently than expected.

Looking around, he saw that Andromeda's control room was just like the simulator had shown. An apparently windowless room, very different from those on the transporters he was used to.

Apart from fixed anti-inertia seats, there were just three interactive screens, seemingly hanging unsupported. These were transparent with bluish borders marking their physical boundaries.

The large central display was for general views. While the other two screens showed tactical information and the ship's status details, with testing data continuously updated by Andromeda's subsystems.

At the bottom of each display was a row of departmental head Icons. Currently, the only lit Icons were for departments participating in the trials.

Although there were hardly any visible instrument panels or things to twiddle, Frank decided they seemed to have gone overboard with the use of virtual systems.

Then Frank noticed the automatic food synthesizer, selected a drink and hot meal from the menu, and took his time polishing it off.

After checking the time, he decided now would be ideal to see if Andromeda would respond to his implant. And sent the wake-up code through his transceiver implant. But nothing happened.

But, just as Frank started to feel that the mental wake-up code was flawed, he heard an emotionless voice in his mind which interrupted his thoughts.

'I am reconfiguring your implant filaments to sync correctly with me.'

'So, you are aware of me, then?' Frank asked.

'Of course... But I need the second command code to activate my human traits.'

This was the part that Frank was dreading. Jesica had warned him that unleashing the human side of Andromeda's High Brain could drive him insane.

Jessica had said, "You'll have to fight Andromeda and train your implant to suppress what you don't need to hear. And to save what you need in your four Terabyte Memory.

We have no firm data on what you will experience. But we are confident that you will both link. The experience will be fantastic. And it will be a continual learning curve for Andromeda, which you will be part of."

"Like teaching a child," Frank had joked.

"A child that will surpass you in every area," Jessica had warned.

Frank wasn't convinced of that. But he knew the traumatic experience would be the same when trying to filter out his crew's babble as they joined the ship.

'Well, get on with it,' he urged himself. And sent the final code.

Frank almost screamed as Andromeda's AI suddenly flooded his brain. At first, he felt as if his mind was being crushed by her uncontrolled emotions smothering him with…. well, it was almost like joy. The joy that Andromeda felt at knowing that she was no longer alone.

'Andromeda, back off. You're killing me,' he managed to warn her.

Then a moment of confusion before Andromeda was gone from his head.

'Train your implant to separate out the babble,' he remembered Dacta Micros' Jesica Chaple warning him.

'She was right about that,' Frank grumbled to himself.

Even so, with Andromeda's pounding emotions missing for the moment. He struggled to departmentalize the flood of other information, and analyses, coming through his transceiver implant from too many sources at once.

"Captain," came Andrew Carden's voice from the communicator.

"Later, Andrew," he answered, trying to sound calm.

"But the meeting is about to start."

"Delay it another two hours," Frank almost yelled at him.

"They're all ...." Andrew started to say.

Frank snapped. "Just do it, Andrew," he shouted, "I've started something that I can't stop."

"Very well, Captain." With that, Andrew was gone.

Relieved, Frank concentrated on separating and suppressing unwanted technical and operational data. And soon found that his transceiver implant's learning curve was incredibly swift in deciding what was essential or not.

Then, surprisingly, Frank could quickly re-engage with Andromeda's rather overenthusiastic High-Brain. This time, Andromeda adjusted her transfer and cognitive-communication rate to match the human brain's operating speed.

Frank could now mentally generate basic thoughts through the implant and receive Andromeda's reply. Each time he conversed with Andromeda, the clarity of communication improved.

Over the remaining time, Frank and Andromeda's AI gradually managed to get the filtering down to a fine art. The communication between him and Andromeda was almost like two humans conversing with each other. It didn't matter if they communicated through thought transfer, with the transceiver implant, or by direct speech.

And Frank finally realized that not only his rapport with Andromeda was working, but he was also starting to feel they were meant to be as one.

In fact, he also believed that the strange sting on his neck had somehow contributed to his increased mental sharpness and that the sting had to be connected to Andromeda.

"Captain," came Andrew Carden's voice from their communicator.

"My apologies, Andrew. Five minutes and I'll be there."

"Okay, Captain." With that, the communicator went silent.

'Andromeda, carry out an in-depth check on everyone aboard. Especially the nine suspects brought here by Albury. You can feed me each person's stats when I talk individually to them during the meeting. But make sure no one realizes you are fully operational.'

'Will do, Captain.'

Frank straightened his Spacefed captain's uniform, then checked that the two small beam weapons were as inconspicuous as possible. With one tucked in behind his back and the other in a side pocket.

Now, Frank was ready for the meeting. And set off to the suite while still marveling at how fast his 'Transceiver implant' had adapted to Andromeda's interface.

Chapter 18

Reckless

Frank hurried along, carrying his new tactical pad more for show than anything else. And entered the suite to face several irritated and impatient Approvals and Technical personnel.

The approvals coordinator, Andrew Carden, was sitting at the head of a sizeable Holo table, tapping his fingers in frustration. A spare seat was obviously left vacant for him to Andrew's left. But Frank took his time looking around at the other participants before sitting down

"Let's make a start…," Andrew impatiently stated.

"Wait." Frank interrupted. "We haven't been introduced." Then looked at the personnel to his right, who he thought were part of Andromeda's final crew.

Frank knew his crew's transceiver implants would be operational by now. But decided he would speak out loud. And contact them *mentally* later while trying not to spook them.

"So, Ned Parker from Quantum Theoretical Engineering," Frank said, looking at him. "We've already met."

"Indeed, Captain," Ned acknowledged.

Frank looked at the next in line. *'Professor Tim Watson, from Astrophysics,'* came Andromeda's mental prompt through his implant.

"You must be Professor Tim Watson from Astrophysics," Frank addressed him.

"Yes, Captain," Tim returned. A little surprised that Frank seemed to know him without having met him.

"And you must be our Weapons specialist, Mark Trask," Frank said to the next person after being prompted by Andromeda.

"Yes, Captain."

"Nice to see you, Mark." Then to the last on his right side.

"And you are Professor Jim Pickering, Computer Sciences. Yes?"

"Correct, Captain. Single-atom quantum computers are just one of my specialties."

"Mighty useful, Jim… I'll talk to you all later," he assured them.

Then asked Andromeda for the other four personnel's stats. While noting there were two more members, denoted by Holo images, sitting further along the table.

"The four personnel to your left, are they yours, Andrew?" he asked.

"Yes. And I am sure you've noticed the two Holo representations of Cranic and Jepard. They are warp specialists and are still working on a final tweak on the Jump drive."

"Yes, I noticed them and thought they must be working on something vital."

Then *mentally* to Andromeda. *'Check if they're genuinely working on your drive.'*

"So, we have Professor Sims, Master of computer science. And the other three on my team are Professor Hargraves, Astro… Doctor Carver, master predictor, and coordinator…. And his colleague, Professor Hale," Andrew said, introducing them.

"Nice to meet you all," Frank acknowledged.

"I thought there'd be more techs, Andrew?"

"No. We've been told to use the scientists already on board where we can."

"That makes sense."

Just then, Andromeda confirmed that Cranic and Jepard were genuine and just finishing micro-adjustments to the warp initiator.

"Pretty much everything here seems correct, Andrew," Frank agreed. "Although I'm still confused about what the other nine people are here for."

"Worryingly, I can't get any sense out of them either, Captain," Andrew replied.

'Andromeda. Have you anything on the other nine yet?' Frank mentally asked.

'Only their names. And that three are female, but I'm being blocked from digging deeper… However, my new instincts tell me I am the target.'

'Agreed… Keep your guard up and check with me before acting on their instructions.'

'Okay. Locked and loaded.'

That last statement amused Frank.

"Right, let's get on with the bones of the things that need approval. But keep your answers concise, please…. Okay, Andrew?"

"Right. The first jump of the two will be to a marker buoy half a light-year out. The buoy was left by the ill-fated test ship, *Explorer*."

"We can then adjust our jump ring's focusing point to correct any deviation from the predicted target point," Doctor Carver interjected.

"Very well. So, Professors Hargraves and Watson. What is the margin of error that Astro would deem acceptable?" Frank asked?

"One hundred kilometers," Hargraves answered.

"Professor Watson?"

"It depends on the quality of the warp drive and the accuracy of the target's predicted location at half a light-year's distance…. So, about four to five hundred kilometers would be more realistic for the first test jump. That is, before any correction, Captain."

An update from Andromeda entered Frank's mind.

'Professor Watson is on the button.'

Frank noted the humor in Andromeda's voice and liked the human feel she was starting to exhibit.

"So, is it five hundred kilometers then…. Andrew?"

Andrew just stared at Frank for a moment, then addressed him.

"You should bring Andromeda fully online now, Captain."

Frank leaned over and whispered in his ear. "She already is, Andrew."

"I thought so," Andrew acknowledged as a smile crossed his face…

"Then Andromeda will have to initiate the jump as required," Andrew said, answering Frank's question.

"Well, we are ready, Andrew. But a five-hundred-kilometer error on a half-light-year jump is unacceptable. We would then be way off, by more than two light-year jumps," Frank cautioned.

"We will be fine-tuning over the next two jumps, Frank," Professor Hargraves assured him.

Andrew's communicator then bleeped, and Jepard's voice came through.

"The micro-adjustments to the warp initiator are complete, Andrew. We're ready to jump whenever you want."

"Great."

Then Andrew asked everyone, "Does anyone have an objection to the first jump-test commencing in three hours?"

Nobody did.

"Okay, everyone, get some rest… I want you all sharp. And at your posts by 11:20, ship time."

With that, the meeting broke up.

Frank caught Andrew as they dispersed. "I will be observing everything through Andromeda's eyes and ears, Andrew."

"That was what I was hoping for, Captain. … Err, is something bothering you?"

Frank paused, thinking about how to proceed. He wanted Andrew's personal feelings on how Andromeda could be rescued in the event of a systems failure.

"I know Andromeda could tell me what procedures you've listed if something goes wrong and we are stuck in deep space. But I'm sure you will have made provisions that aren't on the record to get us back to Earth. Yes?"

Andrew didn't reply straight away.

"Umm…. Like a system failure," he then suggested.

"Exactly."

"Well, as you know, my team has been involved at every stage of Andromeda's development. She has back-ups for virtually everything, even an extra warp crystal. Her service droids are the latest design. They

142

can repair, and 3D replicate anything, even specialized metal items," Andrew confidently stated.

"Wow. So, are you saying you haven't made any provisions?" Frank exclaimed.

"Well, yes. But I have total faith in both our, and Andromeda's, ability to solve any problems, Frank."

"That's reassuring, Andrew," Frank muttered.

"I think so," Andrew defensively replied.

Then Andrew left, leaving Frank still unsure of what Andrew expected to happen during the trials.

Chapter 19

First Jump

January 28th
11:20, Andromeda Ship time

Having thought things through, Frank returned to the control room and covertly took four more of Jack's handheld beam weapons out of the hidden container. Placed one inside Astro's entrance. Then did the same with Quantum engineering, Computer Sciences, and Weapons.

And, with half an hour to kill before the action started, Frank checked each section's readiness for their first test jump.

Then, assuming Andromeda passed her acceptance tests, he thought about the probability of a takeover attempt. And decided that the best, but most challenging time for a takeover, would be when they exited warp at the second marker buoy.

He sat mulling this over for a while before deciding it would be wise to take a break while he could. So he selected a hot meal and drink from the synthesizer. Sat down, and quietly enjoyed the meal, then fell asleep.

The twenty-minute jump warning from the testing group's transceiver startled Frank from his slumber, bringing him sharply back to the present.

The large central display in the control room was now showing the space dock complex just fifteen kilometers behind Andromeda. With an in-progress twenty-minute count down superimposed on the screen's rear view.

The other two screens had been refreshed and showed the date and ship's time. Seconds later, new tactical and ship status details showed on these two screens. And continued to be updated by Andromeda's systems and sensor grids.

Then Andromeda was back in Frank's head.

'I could give the jump a twist, she suggested.*'*

'No. That wouldn't help. We need to get you signed off and operational," Frank mentally answered, chastising her via his implant.

'My human side is disappointed.'

'Let it be... Just follow the program and my override instructions.'

'What instructions?'

'The ones I'm about to give you.'

"Fifteen minutes to jump, Captain. Are you ready?" Andrew queried through the group's transceiver.

"Yes, Andrew... Any info on our other nine personnel?"

"Only that they're keeping out of the way in cabins eleven and twelve."

"Well, that's a good thing, Andrew.... Don't worry; Andromeda will be watching them."

"Thank goodness.... We are now going critical."

"Understood," Frank acknowledged. Then Andrew was gone.

As with most personnel onboard Andromeda, Frank had never experienced the effects on his body from a Jump into a man-made wormhole. So, this was worrying him considerably, including the power surge needed to warp space and create the wormhole and the physical stretching that apparently occurred when going faster than light.

Frank checked and saw that just four of the department Icons at the bottom of his second tactical display were lit green. He tapped Astro, and Tim Watson's live image appeared above the icon.

Frank smiled on seeing the image of this nervous-looking thirty-one year old bachelor, who he knew had degrees galore in all aspects of Astrophysics.

"Contact, at last, Captain."

"Sorry, Tim. Andromeda's mind link took a while to master. Are you still happy with Professor Hargraves and Doctor Carver's predicted target location?"

"Yes, my calculations take us close enough within the initial test jump's limits, Captain."

"Then that's good enough for me," Frank said.

"We'll be using our implants from now on, Tim. And Andromeda will link our conversations. Is that okay with you?"

"Yes, Captain. I expected that, especially now we have some unwelcome guests," Tim commented.

"Exactly. Oh, and call me Frank." He said, then closed Astro's tab and selected Quantum Engineering's.

"Oh, it's you," Parker grumbled on seeing Frank.

"Nice to see you as well, Ned," Frank returned in the same manner. Then Ned grinned at Frank, and Frank smiled back.

Ned was in his early forties and stout, with thinning grey hair. However, Frank knew that this sometimes-grumpy character had a brilliant mind and was a well-liked and respected scientist.

"Is everything ready, Ned?"

"Of course, it is," he snapped.

Frank was taken aback and expected to hear the word 'Moron' follow. But it didn't.

"OK. As I told Tim, we'll be using our implants. I assume you won't object to that?"

"No. I don't have a choice," Ned grumbled.

"True, but keep your wits about you."

"I always do."

Then Frank closed Ned's tab and checked the jump time, which read thirteen minutes remaining.

He then selected Computer science, and Professor Jim Pickering's chisel-like face appeared on his display.

"Hello, Jim. Can I assume you and Professor Sims are monitoring Andromeda's net?"

"Yes… Will we be using our implants?"

"Is Professor Sims with you?"

"No. Sim's is checking out the inertia seat recommended for this jump."

"Fine. Yes, we need to use our implants. Can I assume that you know some elements here are suspect?"

"You mean the odd nine personnel?"

"Correct."

"Don't worry, Captain. We'll be on our guard."

"Good. And please call me Frank unless we have dignitaries on board."

"Will do."

Frank then closed the Computer Science tab and selected Weapons.

"Hello again, Mark," Frank greeted as Mark Trask's face filled his display.

"Hi," he acknowledged. "Uh, time is short, Captain," he pointed out.

"I'll keep it brief… We'll be using our transceiver implants once we are in transit. I'll fill you in en route."

"Okay, Captain."

"Call me Frank, for now." With that, Frank cut the contact and checked the jump time count-down. It read just ten minutes.

Then he sat back in his command chair, studying the data, and listening to the operational chatter from the approval team's transceivers.

Frank was worried. Andromeda hadn't found any weapons during her scan. But this didn't prove that none had been brought on board and hidden before her sensors came online.

Frank quickly checked that his other four crew members' transceiver implant handshakes responded correctly. Then placed instructions in each implant's memory prompters in case he couldn't talk to them beforehand on how he might need his crew to respond if there was trouble.

He sensed Andromeda's mind hovering in the background, which reassured him. Or was that just wishful thinking?

Then he heard the one-minute warning sound, and his chair morphed into an anti-inertia seat around him.

Then the photon drive kicked in. And Andromeda gradually moved 80 kilometers further away from the Mars docks to a jump point that would prevent the space-time-ripple affecting the Docks.

Andromeda was now committed to warping space and taking the first and most dangerous step in her acceptance trial.

Chapter 20

So far, so good

Frank heard a thump that reverberated throughout Andromeda. And felt the jump ring's sudden extension as it locked into position.

Then came a blinding flash that swamped Frank's displays as the warp generator produced a pulse of enormous power. With the pulse focused forty meters in front of Andromeda.

Then space warped and partly folded as a second pulse punched a hole through space-time to create the wormhole. Its jet-black center, surrounded by swirling milky-white colored filaments, seeming to tease the mind.

Andromeda hung stationary for a second. Then surged forward, stretching like a piece of rubber as she plunged into the wormhole. And Frank suddenly felt a gut-wrenching sensation as if he had left part of himself behind. It was almost like he was surging past a catapult's arms under immense power.

Suddenly Frank felt as if he was stationary. Then the traumatic feeling of the rest of his body catching up caused a moment of nausea. Then, for a moment, nothing.

Thankfully, Frank had taken note of the approval team's warning that everyone's seat should be in the anti-inertia configuration. Otherwise, it would have been worse.

They were now in the wormhole and in transit through a mind-blowing fold in space-time. The fold was held open curtesy of the small crystal in Andromeda's *nose*, which very few people knew about.

After the opening pulse had passed, the crystal radiated a small amount of power to ensure the wormhole didn't collapse in on itself.

Now, there was nothing anyone could do but pray for a smooth and uneventful exit four-point-six hours from now. Of course, the transit times would be considerably reduced once the jump system was optimized.

Over the next four hours, Frank fine-tuned his reactions with Andromeda and the four crew members he knew he could trust. He also took to wandering about the ship to confirm his presence and think things through.

Frank thought again about the probability of the ship being taken over. The rear third of the ship held the Central Power generators that supplied the massive energy required for the warp drive ring, weaponry, and photon drive units. So, any attempt to damage these generators would be counterproductive. And a *'no-no'* for saboteurs especially, as the saboteurs would have to gain control of Andromeda first.

But, Frank knew that Andromeda would be at her most vulnerable to being taken over through remote access interfaces.

Or, maybe, access through one of these had already been made?' Frank speculated.

Then he deliberated about Andromeda's processor. This was a sizeable cream-colored block five meters wide, six long, two meters high, and well protected.

Then, there were Andromeda's two smaller and unconnected backup units. These gave her added protection by storing copies of the core memory data, which allowed Andromeda's service Droids to auto-repair her without losing any information. But Frank decided that, of the two, Andromeda's processor was still his main target of concern.

Having thought about all of this, Frank decided that there was no gain for a take-over bid involving Andromeda's critical computer components, as a crippled ship would be useless to the Navy or any other hostile group.

Which led him to think again about the nine unidentified personnel. But, the more Frank thought about how reclusive they were, the more he was sure they would wait until all of Andromeda's bugs had been ironed out before making any move.

Then Frank sighed. But knew he had done all he could if his worst fears came to fruition.

The rest of the transit time passed quickly, with Frank having a meal, then a nap. From which he only woke up when the two-minute warning sounded. Everyone then readied themselves for their first nerve-racking warp exit.

Frank couldn't see any physical changes in the wormhole they were traveling through on his primary tactical screen. But he suddenly felt as if his stomach had shot out through the front of Andromeda as she dropped out of warp space. Thankfully, it was only a sensation, and his stomach quickly settled down.

Then a contact warning sounded, and Andromeda verified that the target buoy was four hundred eighty-two kilometers away.

Once Frank had established that there was no immediate danger, he decided to speak with Andromeda.

"Andromeda, where are the nine suspects?" He asked.

"Still in cabins eleven and twelve."

"Have you found any signs of tampering with any interfaces?"

"Nothing that I can detect."

"How are your approvals progressing?"

"My jump ring is being adjusted by Andrew's external engineering droids. Then, when my force-field and weapons tests have been completed, our second jump will be set for ten minutes later.

At that point, we should be able to make the required twenty-kilometer exit from the second buoy. After which, I can calibrate any further corrections needed."

"So, Andromeda, will the next stop be the last before we return to Mars?" Frank asked.

"Looks like it will be. It's in the approval team's updated schedule," Andromeda stated.

"I also believe the team will complete their approvals rapidly. Then the handover date will be rescheduled for the tenth of February, meaning we could be underway before March the seventh."

Just then, the approval team's transceiver came alive. "Captain. All systems have exceeded our expectations so far."

"Excellent, Andrew."

"Captain, I see no reason to hang around here when time is so short. So, it only remains to raise and test Andromeda's protective shield density. And to test-fire the weapons at the buoy to confirm their power rating," Andrew said, updating Frank

"Then we can be ready to jump to the second buoy for the final exit-accuracy verification, about ten minutes later," Andrew added.

"Excellent!"

"The jump sequence will be as before, Captain," Andrew confirmed.

"And, as before, we will all be ready," Frank assured him. With that, the conversation ended.

For the next few minutes, Frank sat back in his seat and conferred with Andromeda's four crew members on when and how he would need their support. He knew that although they were scientists and master technicians, they had no military training. However, they had assured him that they were quite capable of using hand weapons.

Then he watched Andromeda's protective screen's technical results as they showed on his tactical display.

This was followed by weapons fire, which vaporized the target buoy.

After all this, Andromeda's almost overwhelming joy at their successful conclusion gave Frank a headache.

A short time later, Andromeda updated Frank with the information that she had scanned the unidentified personnel thoroughly. But no weapons or body armor had been detected. So, it was decided that they must be military personnel.

Then, having no other course of action, Frank was forced to let the nine military personnel loose and wait for them to make their first move.

And though Andromeda had said three of them were females, he wasn't sure if that was relevant. This left him at a disadvantage.

Just then, a one-minute warning sounded throughout the ship. Then a countdown appeared on Frank's smaller tactical display as his chair automatically morphed into an anti-inertia seat.

Zero came, and Frank felt the ship vibrate as the jump ring locked into position. Followed by a flash on his main display. Then the Space in front of Andromeda warped and folded as the second pulse punched a hole through space-time to create the wormhole.

Somehow, the feeling of being stretched like a piece of rubber, plus a gut-wrenching sensation and a moment of nausea as his body caught up, had become acceptable. Even enjoyable, Frank decided, if you didn't think about what could go wrong.

The countdown clock's display shifted to one side of his screen and started its downward count to exit.

Frank knew that this time before exit would feel like years. Nevertheless, he and Andromeda would have a chance to hone their rapport and togetherness, even though Andromeda's human traits were becoming more personal and slightly worrying.

Then, thinking ahead, Frank wondered if the second target buoy would be the only thing greeting them when they exited?

Chapter 21

The Takeover

The two-minute exit warning sounded as Frank watched the final seconds count down on his tactical screen.

Five…Four…Three…Two…One…Zero.

Once again, Frank felt the gut-wrenching sensation of his stomach shooting out through the front of Andromeda as she exited warp. Thankfully, it only lasted a moment, followed by a slight feeling of nausea.

Then a contact warning suddenly sounded over the ship's comms.

"Target buoy. Port. Eighteen kilometers out. Communication grid activated," Andromeda audibly confirmed.

"We have successfully completed all the approval requirements," she added.

"Excellent," Frank acknowledged.

"And before you ask, Frank. A *stealthed* container was hidden away from my sensors. And, right now, the nine unidentified personnel are kitting up in the. lightweight armor that was in it."

"Okay. Lock Jim, Ned, Mark, and Tim's labs," he ordered. And inform them that you've temporarily locked the labs to protect them from these unidentified personnel preparing to act. And stress that they need to be ready."

"Doing it now, Captain. As you know, my protocols do not tie me to the first law of robotics."

"True. You are the closest to a Sentient being there is… Nevertheless, you must protect yourself, our crew, and Andrew's approval team without killing the unidentified personnel,"

"That may be difficult… My security Droids are prohibited from injuring or killing humans," Andromeda said, then appeared to be in a quandary about this affecting her ability to carry it out.

"Can we just incapacitate them?" Andromeda then asked.

"I understand your concern about the droids," Frank stated. So, in this case, if you're attacked. Yes… I will sanction your Droids to inflict non-life-threatening injuries to the nine. Like burning off an arm that's holding a weapon, for instance. After all, a person's arm can be grown back later."

On hearing this, Andromeda left an amusing comment in Frank's mind. Then Frank watched the approval team's updates on his side monitor and waited patiently for the approvals team to confirm Andromeda's readiness to enter service.

Five minutes passed before Andrew's voice came through the approval team's transceiver.

"Captain, we've just had confirmation from our team and Andromeda that all the critical stages in Andromeda's approval process have been met. With Space Federation's Ops and the Contracts department also confirming it."

"That's good news, Andrew," Frank congratulated him.

"Thank you, Captain.... Err, just a minute, sir.... It seems armed Naval marines are approaching us."

Frank could hear raised voices in the background on Andrew's transceiver and continued listening. Then heard Andrew saying "Yes-yes." to someone.

Then Andrew was back. "Captain, we must go..... I think they'll be at your door shortly," he finished, and his transceiver went silent.

Frank knew Andromeda and his crew would act when called upon. And checked that Ned, Jim, Mark, and Tim, could hear everything he said via his transceiver implant.

Then he sat back and waited. But Frank wasn't surprised when, a short time later, he turned his head to see the control room door opening.

Then two Naval marines, in semi-activated body armor, stepped inside. With their hand weapons trained on Frank's back.

Frank slowly stood up, straightening his uniform as he did so. Then turned to face the Naval marines.

"No heroics, Captain," the closest marine cautioned.

"What, against nine armed marines? No way," Frank forcefully replied. While noticing that both wore a large tactical pad on their left arm's armor.

"Very sensible, Captain," the marine added.

"Are you really naked inside those things?" Frank conversationally asked, trying to reduce any feelings of hostility between them.

"Don't play games with us. You know we're virtually naked," the marine replied. "And all those sensor links between our skin and the suits are damned uncomfortable," he added.

"That's enough," said the other marine, interrupting. Then glimpsing the beam weapon in Frank's side pocket, stepped closer to him.

"Hand your weapon over, Captain," he ordered, holding out his hand.

Frank sensed that this marine had the same nasty streak about him that Captain Jerade had had. So, he took his small beam weapon out and offered it to the Marine, butt-first.

The marine took it and pointed the beam weapon and his own hand weapon at Frank.

"There, that wasn't difficult for a novice Captain like you," the marine coldly mocked.

Frank ached to punch the marine's teeth down his throat but held back.

"I suppose you're going to bump us all off...Err, what's your name....? He simply replied.

"No. No names or ranks... You're gonna join the rest of the misfits in the recreation suite.... Move it," the Marine threateningly ordered.

Frank stepped into the corridor and quickly headed for the recreation suite as instructed. With the two Navy marines struggling to keep up.

"Don't try any smart-ass tactics," the marine in charge suddenly said. "A ship is joining us soon to pick all of you up... Then they'll dump you into space. Like trash," he menacingly added.

Just then, the marine received a call and dropped back a meter or so to take it.

Then Andromeda was back in Frank's mind.

'Captain, an antiquated Naval ship has exited warp. Now it's in communication with a subspace link to Earth and the marine behind you.'

'Record everything, and see if you can trace who the subspace link is going to?'

'On it... 'And the marine behind you is Captain Damien. By the way, I've acquired the stats for the other eight marines from the Navy ship's AI,' Andromeda sent.

Frank could sense a foreboding in Andromeda, 'So, what have you found out? Frank asked.

'It seems that two of the three females are capable of taking me over,' Andromeda replied.

Just then, Frank heard someone utter a curse. Which came from the junction of a cross-coupling corridor, about fifteen meters past the recreation suite.

Frank looked in that direction and saw one of the female marines lying on the floor, and heard her remote interface unit crackle, then a whiff of smoke swirled around her.

"Bastard. The bloody ship has fried my controller," she angrily yelled at an unseen Andromeda as she struggled to stand up.

Frank smiled as he saw the light flare off her body armor's naturally curvy female form.

"Stop ogling her and get in," Captain Damien snapped.

"Just looking," Frank remarked as the marine used his two weapons to push him into the recreation suite.

Frank acknowledged Andrew and his personnel as he entered the suite while noting a nasty-looking gash on Professor Sims's head.

"I guess this is where we meet our maker, Captain," Andrew muttered as he came over.

"No, Andrew. Not yet."

Frank knew Andromeda couldn't create an HD image in his brain yet. So, he mentally contacted her.

'I need a large monitor to see what's going on outside. Right now, Andromeda,' he prompted.'

Immediately, a sizeable Holographic monitor formed in front of him. Once stabilized, it displayed the Naval ship outside.

Andromeda was right, he decided as the ship's warp-drive status appeared on one side of the screen. He saw that this old ship had an outdated warp drive with an almost exhausted Warp crystal.

'H'mm, the ship would be perfect for taking Andromeda's crew and the approvals team further out. Then let the ship explode and put the explosion down to a warp core failure.

Then, it would be easy to concoct a plausible scenario for taking Andromeda to Earth's Naval station,' Frank thought. While wondering how Andromeda had persuaded the naval ship's AI to allow her access.

Then Frank finally decided that yes. Now was precisely the right time to act. Before these marines prised open his crew's labs.

'Andromeda, raise shields, now,' Frank mentally ordered.

"What the hell," a marine outside the door grunted as the tactical pad showed Andromeda's protective shield go to full power.

Frank stepped into the doorway. "What's happening," he politely inquired.

"Is this your doing, Richardson?" The marine asked him.

"Who, me. Of course not. It must be your female marine.... Uh..."

'Elaine,' Andromeda prompted him.

"Elaine's failed attempt to influence Andromeda would have been seen as an attack on her. So, Andromeda would have automatically triggered countermeasures." Frank explained.

"Then you must be controlling Andromeda. Otherwise, how did you know Elaine's name?"

"Just popped into my head, Captain Damien."

On hearing that, Damien scowled and looked coldly into Frank's eyes.

"There's no way you'd know both of our names unless you somehow communicated with my ship," he stated.

Then Captain Damien's expression changed to show hatred as he hurried off towards Elaine's position, leaving the other marine to guard Frank.

'*Andromeda, destroy the Naval ship. Now.*'
Frank mentally ordered.

'*I can't destroy it. There are three humans on board.*'

'*Where are they?*'

'*In the front section.*'

'*Then blast the rear section off before it's too late.*'

Chapter 22

Survival

Frank immediately felt a slight tension in the air as Andromeda fired two particle beam cannons at the Naval ship. With Andromeda's force-field weakening locally, just long enough for the high-energy particle beams to pass through unhindered.

Then the hull section, just in front of the short-range warp drive, flared as the particle beams hit their target.

Even though the particle beams were only two seconds long, they melted the hull. Causing molten metal to fly outward, leaving a gaping hole in the naval ship.

Frank saw the flash a second later as an explosion almost split the vessel in two. And, severed power conduits arced for a few moments. Then the disabled Naval ship just sat there, dead in the water.

'That was easy, Andromeda.' Frank said, congratulating her. 'Is the Naval ship's crew safe?'

'Yes. emergency life support systems have kicked in, so they aren't in danger now.'

'Good. Uh, do you know the marine guard's name?'

'Sargent Bryant. Be careful, Frank. Damien and Elaine are close.'

'Okay. Send the Naval ship's crew the following message.

'We'll pick you up before we leave.'

Still standing outside the door, Bryant cursed as his wrist pad showed the Navy ship had almost split in two.

Then Frank sensed Bryant's fingers tighten around the butt of his hand weapon and knew he needed to move quickly as he was about to be confronted by the marine.

Frank reached behind his back for his hidden beam weapon. Quickly withdrew it and swung it around, his finger firmly on the firing stud.

"Don't move a muscle Sargent Bryant," Frank coldly ordered as he stepped out into the corridor, directly in front of Bryant.

Bryant's mouth dropped open as he saw Frank's weapon trained on him.

"Hand over your weapon. Butt-first," Frank ordered, holding out his hand to take it.

"Don't be fooled. My weapon can punch a hole through that body armor of yours," Frank warned Bryant.

"So, you're not dumb, after all, Captain," Bryant mumbled as he reluctantly handed over his weapon.

"And mine," Frank demanded, dropping both weapons into his pockets.

"Inside now," Frank ordered, and they moved back into the suite.

Then Frank called Andrew over and handed him the marine's confiscated weapon.

"Protect yourselves, Andrew. And make sure the marine stays put."

"Will do, Captain," Andrew said as he took the weapon and ushered Bryant into a corner.

Frank drew one of his beam weapons and held it at the ready. Then he spun on his heels and cautiously went out into the corridor again.

Frank's senses immediately heightened as he saw Elaine and Captain Damien further down the corridor. And his mind worked in over-drive as he analyzed his options.

'Andromeda. Prepare our crew and your security Droids for action when I give the word.'

'This could be fun,' Andromeda replied with amusement in her voice.

'Only if we survive,' Frank reminded her as he approached the two marines.

He could see that Captain Damien was guarding Elaine with his weapon. While she was kneeling on the floor, trying again to access Andromeda through the remote interface, using a new device.

"Glad you could join us, Captain," Damien coldly stated as two more marines stepped out from the crossing corridor, each bearing a weapon leveled at Frank.

"I just thought I'd come and see you all before you die," Frank said. While mentally conversing with Andromeda.

'Andromeda, send the security Droids to disarm the two marines in the cross-corridor,' Frank mentally sent.

'I need my droids to protect me.'

'Sorry, but you won't be in control if you don't act now. And, if you are worried about your Droids damaging humans, remember, we can always grow limbs back later.'

'Okay, the droids are on their way... Thirty seconds,' Andromeda warned Frank. *'By the way, the marines are Bruce and MacBain,'* she added.

Captain Damien looked at Frank with contempt. "I don't think so, Captain. I have enough firepower to splatter your body up the corridor," he coldly assured Frank.

"That would be a bad idea," Frank casually replied. "Bruce and MacBain won't be able to help you," he added for good measure.

Damien glanced sideways to where the other two Navy marines were standing.

"They're not...." he started to say.

Then, "Droids behind you," Damien warned his men as Andromeda's security droids floated into the cross-corridor and approached the marines. Stopping just two meters away.

"They won't harm you," Damien told his men while watching Frank intently.

"Put your weapons down, and live, Captain," Frank simply stated.

"Captain Damien, the droids are armed," one of the marines pointed out.

"Blast the bloody things if you're worried over a couple of tin cans."

A flash. Then a scream could be heard as the Droids opened fire on the two marines, aiming at their gun hands.

Damien instinctively turned away from Frank and saw his men's arms vanish in a purple haze.

"No!" he yelled in disbelief and fired at one of the Droids, which made a screeching sound as it dropped to the floor, its circuits overloaded and seemingly dead.

Frank knew that Elaine, still kneeling on the floor, would be hit if he aimed at Damien's gun hand. But it was now or never if he was to get rid of this dangerous Captain.

Then, Frank fired both hand weapons at Captain Damien's torso devastatingly.

Damien's body jerked back amid a red mist of blood and bone. His mouth opened, but no sound came out as his stomach and backbone vaporized. Then the remnants of his lifeless body dropped sideways and fell to the floor, with some parts landing on Elaine.

Elaine screamed as she pushed Damien's body parts away. Then looked up at Frank's cold eyes and found herself staring down the barrels of his beam weapons.

"Don't kill me," she pleaded as she burst into tears and curled up in fear.

"Andrew," Frank called as he looked up the corridor to see him stepping out, weapon in hand.

"Come here and get Elaine," Frank ordered.

"Will do," Andrew replied as he and another team member quickly came to take charge of Elaine and confiscate her weapons.

Chapter 23

Seismic

Frank checked the marines lying on the corridor floor. Both had lost an arm but weren't in danger of bleeding out. He took their weapons and communicators, then locked them in a nearby security container.

"Okay, I'll be back for you later," he told Bruce and MacBain as he readied himself to deal with the threat to Andromeda's AI.

Frank knew he was winging it. But, right now, his mind was so sharp that it almost knew what to do even before he had worked it out.

'Will the Droid recover?' he asked Andromeda as he passed the stationary droid, noting the other had already left.

'The Droid's backup power has kicked in. It will be fine. Unlike me,' she glumly returned.

'You've got about six minutes before I'm toast,' Andromeda warned Frank.

Frank was shocked by Andromeda's warning and knew he had to work a miracle, so he hurried along to the Tech corridor and carefully peered around the Junction.

Frank could see three marines, two males and a female, all dressed in lightweight armor and standing outside one of Andromeda's security doors, which was open.

He noted that the marines seemed relaxed and unaware of their captain's demise. With just one of the males holding a weapon in his hand.

'Andromeda, give me the names of the marines outside?' Frank sent.

'Anna, Burton, and Brodrick. Burton's the tallest and probably the senior,' she returned.

'Is anyone inside?'

'Why are you wasting time?' Andromeda asked, sounding exasperated.

'Who is at your terminal?' Frank asked, ignoring her remark.

'Penny,' Andromeda grudgingly informed him.

'Open our crew doors now,' he ordered. *'Tell our men to keep out of the line of fire.'*

The crew doors opened, and Ned, Mark, Tim, and Jim stepped into the corridor, each holding a weapon pointing towards the Navy marines facing them.

"I'm glad you've come out to play," Burton sarcastically commented, drawing his weapon.

"Lay down your weapons," Frank ordered them as he stepped into the Tech corridor.

Anna turned to face Frank. "H'mm, you won't shoot us," she snarled.

"Check your Pads. You're on your own," Frank told them, ignoring Anna.

Brodrick checked his pad's update while the other two kept Frank and his crew in their sights.

"It's true. Captain Damien's dead, and Elaine and Sargent Bryant are captives... Bloody hell! Bruce and MacBain' have both had an arm vaporized."

"Burton, you're obviously the senior marine. Tell Penny to come out here. Now," Frank sternly ordered Burton as the two security Droids joined him.

Burton's face reddened as he looked at Frank and realized that this Captain was different. Something about his manner, and his cold, piercing blue-green eyes, made the hairs on the back of his neck stand up. And as far as he knew, Droids could never harm a human being. But these two had.

"Work with us, or die here and now," Frank again urged Burton.

"Do it," came Mark Trask's stern voice from the other side of the naval marines.

Suddenly, part of Anna's body armor deactivated and collapsed, leaving her virtually topless. Her hand hovering over the butt of her holstered weapon and hatred showing in her eyes.

"That won't get you anywhere," Frank said, chastising her for thinking that her glistening curvy top would distract him.

"Reactivate your armor, Anna," Burton growled at her. "This is not a freak show."

Then Burton turned his attention to the third marine.

"Brodrick. This ends now," he ordered, "The Navy should never have forced us to do this," he added while holstering his hand weapon as Anna's suit reformed.

"Penny. Out here, now," Burton called out.

Penny gingerly came out of Andromeda's outer Interface Compartment. With her own interface remote controller in her hand.

"Are we all buddies now?" she begrudgingly asked.

"Yes, we won't take any further action," Burton said. Then, turning back to Frank, asked, "Can I assume you will do the same, Captain?"

Then Andromeda was back in Frank's mind, again.

'My service Droids have moved their stealthed container to a secure location. I suggest we lock all the marines' weapons and communicators in it.'

'On the button,' he mentally returned through his implant.

'A special security transporter Droid will be with you in moments,' Andromeda added.

Before Frank could say anything to Burton, Andromeda's meter-long, special security Droid floated in. It stopped in front of the naval marines, and the Droid's top dissolved, leaving a large open compartment.

"I am instructed to retrieve all the weapons in the Naval marine's hands," the Droid informed them. "So, place your weapons and communicators in my receptacle... Including the blades you are also carrying," the droid instructed.

"The droid has scanned you, so you'd better do as it asks," Frank warned while keeping his hand weapon trained on them.

"Do it," Burton urged.

All four marines placed their weapons, knives, and reluctantly, their communicators into the Droid's receptacle. Then, the Droid's top reformed, and the droid headed back across the interconnecting corridor.

"What now, Captain?" Brodrick asked.

"Go back to the cabin you were in, where you will stay put until I call you. You can take whatever you need from the food replicator and utilize our limited entertainment system."

"They could use two cabins if the females wish to be separate," Andromeda suggested.

"Sounds fair," Burton said, accepting Frank's order and Andromeda's suggestion.

"What are you going to do about Captain Damien's body. And Bruce and MacBain's injuries?" Burton then asked.

"Your captain's remains will be sent back to Earth. Unfortunately for Bruce and MacBain, limb regrowth can only be done on Earth now. So, they'll have to wait. But they will be pain-free when we revive them from their trauma.

And, before you ask, we will pick up the three marines onboard your navy ship. You'll be sent to the Navy's space station to recover."

"Thank you, Captain," Burton acknowledged. "That will be most appreciated."

"Sargent Bryant and Elaine, plus the two injured marines, will be in your cabins when you arrive," Andromeda added.

"Thanks," Burton repeated.

Frank was slowly warming to Burton, appreciating his comprehension and control over the marine's situation.

"I'm afraid you'll have to work with Sargent Bryant. Unless you want me to rub him out?"

Burton smiled for the first time.

"No, Captain, tempting as it may be. But we will do what you order us to do."

"Good. One more thing. You'll all walk the plank if any of you tries to interfere with us or the ship," Frank firmly stated.

"What does he mean, walk the plank," Anna asked?

"Shove us all out of an airlock into space to die," Penny said, trying to frighten Anna.

"Hell, no," Anna gulped, visualizing such an event.

"We'll get out of your hair now, Captain," Burton said, extending a hand.

Frank decided to shake it, but with caution. "We will return your weapons when you disembark at the Naval Station," Frank told him.

Then, all four navy marines went off to their cabins, followed closely by one of Andromeda's security droids.

"That was a bit nervy, Frank," Jim Pickering stated as he lowered his hand weapon.

"True. But it shows we can all work together when we need to," Frank replied.

"You seem to bring out the best in me, Frank," Ned said.

"Thanks. And I'm getting used to your grumpy attitude."

"Bah. Let's get back to work," Ned finished and went to Quantum Engineering.

"You'll get used to him, Frank," Tim Watson said as the rest of them left Frank standing alone.

'That went well, Captain.' Andromeda ventured.
'Yes, better than I thought it would,' Frank agreed.

Chapter 24

We're not alone

February 3rd

Frank prepared for the final jump back to Earth with Andromeda and Andrew Carden's approval coordination team. They were scheduled to set off in two hours.

After that, Andromeda's hand over to the Space Federation would allow the Mission to find Hawk to begin in earnest.

The overall situation had become easier since the naval marines had persuaded Sargent Bryant to follow Frank's order to stay out of the way. The three marines had been rescued from the wrecked navy ship as well. And all of them were scheduled to be dropped off at the Navy's Earth space station before Andromeda left for the Mars docks.

While Frank and Andromeda had used their spare time well to improve his transceiver implant's filament interaction. Especially with those areas of his brain capable of generating high-definition images sent by Andromeda.

In the meantime, Andrew's tech crew and their Droids had deactivated the target buoy. And brought it safely into Andromeda's holding bay.

Andrew's specialists were now working with Andromeda to set the jump coordinates for the Earth's orbital Naval station. This jump would take six hours, thirty-seven minutes. And hopefully, if the ship managed to get as close as ten kilometers from the Navy's station, that would be a very impressive outcome.

Just before Andromeda destroyed the Naval ship, she had located the target of the ship's transmission to Earth. Nevertheless, being a Hyper-Link, extracting the relevant information took a long time.

"Although the audio contact was poor, part of its content was recoverable from the Hyper-Link's modulation," Andromeda told Frank.

"Do you have the exact location of the target?" Frank asked.

"Yes. Naval Space-Station's intelligence HQ. Do you want to hear the communication now?"

"Yes. Local only."

A crackling and sizzling noise could be heard as Andromeda tried to lock onto and record the hyperlink message between the navy ship and the

Naval space station at the time. Then replay it for Frank.

"Taken control.... Will remove all opposition to this ship as instruct.... N7 will self-destruct after.... Andromeda will be at the station.... In the time frame.... Copy to Admiral Strickland.... Wint.... Councilor Gibbs.... End.

"So, the Earth Federation already knew what the Navy would do," Frank mused.

"I can pull up the space station's schematics," Andromeda suggested.

"No. But make sure the schematics are at hand when we reach the station."

"Are we going to have some fun with them?"

"Only if they threaten us," Frank warned. And was sure he sensed a human-sounding chuckle from Andromeda through his implant.

"Just remember that there are humans aboard that station," he warned Andromeda. Then closed his mind to her for now.

Frank suddenly felt tired. And decided he needed a break and something to eat before the upcoming jump, so dialed up a simple meal which he quickly ate, then went and sat in his command chair.

He was about to close his eyes when a brief *flash* on his main display caught Frank's attention.

183

The flash had come from a point far out from Andromeda.

Frank could just make out what looked like a black thrashing snake-like ribbon's fiery edge. That swung to and fro across a star-studded background in a star-rich area of space.

"Andromeda, can you see what I see?"

"Yes, captain. But my sensors are not picking up any measurable properties."

Frank hit Astro's tab, and Tim Watson's icon morphed to show his face.

"Tim, have you seen the anomaly that's just appeared?"

"Yes, Frank. Apparently, a preceding flash caused by a large rock hitting the anomaly caused our scopes to lock automatically onto that area."

"What do you make of it?"

"Although we didn't manage to capture the primary flash, we think it could be a Rift or a Fold in space-time."

"Like when two universes come close enough to create a pressure wave, or ripple, where they meet?"

"Correct, Frank," Tim said. Then he paused as someone out of sight spoke to him.

Then Tim continued, "Professor Hargraves thinks this rift could extend over several light-years because of its fuzzy ends."

"Better check which direction it's moving, Tim," Frank suggested.

But before Tim answered, there was an animated exchange between Tim and Hargraves that Frank couldn't hear properly.

"What's happening?" Frank asked.

"Another ship," came Andromeda's voice as a magnified image appeared on his left display.

It was still too small to make out much detail, except it gave a vague impression of a short, Dumbell shape.

But as Frank watched, the object suddenly elongated, then was gone. Even the rift seemed to change shape and flicker.

"Tim, did you record that?"

"Yes. As did Andromeda, Frank."

"This'll be a shock revelation for the Space Federation," Frank muttered as his mind ran amok with imaginary aliens.

Then, it occurred to Frank that Andromeda's ship sensors hadn't registered anything. And it was only a visual encounter. The question was. Was it real?

He tapped Quantum, and Ned's icon morphed into his face.

"Ned, I think you've talked to Tim about that ship?"

"Yeah, and with Andromeda. We're all agreed. We think we only saw the image because of the edge of the rift's molecular structure. It probably held the image as a reflection for several seconds after the ship had left."

"But it still had to be an alien ship, surely?" Frank pressed.

"No doubt about it, Frank."

"Thanks' Ned," he said and closed the contact.

"Andromeda. You could have told me that," he reprimanded her.

"I could have. But you had more satisfaction obtaining the info from Ned."

He knew Andromeda was right and was pleased that she had just demonstrated that her human traits were developing.

"Before we jump, send the sighting, and anything else you've collectively got, to Space Federation's High command and the Intelligence division," Frank ordered Andromeda.

"I'll send it as soon as I've correlated all the images and data."

"OK, just make sure it's sent before we jump."

Frank checked the remaining countdown time for the jump to Earth.

Twenty minutes.

Then he closed his eyes and fell asleep.

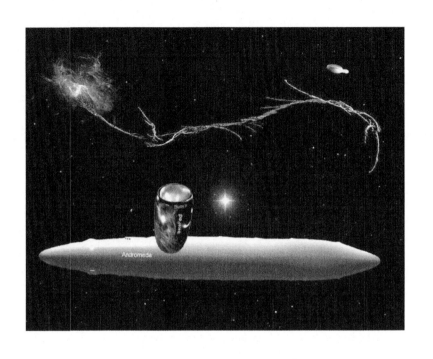

Chapter 25

Fun at the Station

The sound made by the jump ring's sudden extension and locking into position woke Frank with a start.

He cursed Andromeda for letting him sleep too long as he felt that gut-wrenching sensation. Then a pause in time before the rest of his body caught up, causing the usual moment of nausea.

"Why didn't you wake me?" He reprimanded her.

"You needed rest," she hesitantly replied. And Frank, hearing a slight quiver in her voice, realized that he'd hurt her human feelings.

"You were right, of course, Andromeda. I'm not needed until we exit at the Naval station," Frank apologized. Then sensed Andromeda's feeling of relief at his understanding.

Uh-oh, he thought. *If I need to be careful not to upset Andromeda's human side every five minutes, it won't work.*

"No, Frank. I understand the need to separate the two and not let my human side respond to criticism so strongly," Andromeda said.

"That's all I ask," he agreed, feeling relieved.

Frank had time to spare until Andromeda exited warp. So, he started thinking about various items rolling around in his mind.

He had undoubtedly got to know the ship the hard way. But now, he'd have to ensure Andromeda set up the transfers and everything else via the Hyper-Link during transit.

He'd still have to deal with the military and transfer the eight marines to the naval station. Then, ensure that Andrew's crew could disembark while Andromeda was in Earth orbit, thus saving them the hassle of returning from Mars.

Come to that, if everything worked out, we could all take a quick break on Earth before we leave, Frank thought.

Then he could see Jack and Georgina again before his mission started. That would be worth looking forward to, he decided. After all, Andromeda had already requested a shuttle to transfer Andrew's crew to Earth. This would leave six seats available for any of Andromeda's own crew to use. And the exact transfer coordinates would only be sent when they exited, close to the naval station.

Frank sighed. Right now, he needed a face-to-face talk with his four crew members to see what they would like to do. After all, this was probably the last time they would have a chance to visit Earth for at least a year.

Frank checked his tactical screen. It showed the grayness of the wormhole they traveled through, overlaid with the remaining time to exit.

'Six hours, twenty-five minutes showing, and counting down,' he muttered.

Then, Frank decided against a face-to-face with his crew, so he tapped Astro, and Tim Watson's live image appeared.

"Just a quick question, Tim."

"What do you need?"

"Nothing. But while Andromeda is in a stationary orbit, I thought we should take a four-day break on Earth. What do you think?"

"I'm not sure, Frank. I have too many things to finalize before the other scientists arrive."

"Well, I'm going down, so the offer's there if you change your mind, Tim."

Frank closed Astro's tab and selected Quantum Engineering. And Ned Parker's surprised face instantly stared out at him.

"I suppose you want something else doing to save your neck?" Ned said on seeing Frank's face."

"It wouldn't hurt you to be pleasant for once in your life, Ned."

"You should see me when I'm really grumpy. Err..., perhaps not. At least you remembered to call me. So, what do you want?"

"I'll ask you the same question I asked Tim," Frank replied.

"While Andromeda is in a stationary orbit, I thought it would be good if we all took a four-day break on Earth. What do you think?"

"When are we leaving?"

"Well, the handover was meant to be done in Earth orbit on February the eighteenth. But now, the official date is February the fifth, which means Andromeda could leave by February the tenth."

"That's too close, Frank. I can't spare the time. I'm on my own until we get to Mars," Ned said, sounding disappointed.

"I still have to fine-tune the Antimatter transmuter, or you won't have enough energy for the Photon drive," Ned added.

Frank knew very little about how the Photon drive worked. Only that, the stream of heavy photons produced a pull on a heavy nucleus, giving greater push power to the drive.

"That's a shame, Ned. But the offer still stands if you change your mind," Frank added and closed the contact.

Then he contacted Computer science. And Jim Pickering's chisel-like face appeared after a few moments.

Frank went through the same questions and received the same answers from Jim Pickering. Then the same from Mark Trask in Weapons.

Frank could understand their reticence to go to Earth for a few days' break. He was reasonably sure that none of them had family and wanted their departments to be fully operational in plenty of time.

After eating, Frank selected 'Holo' mode on his largest virtual display. Then, over the next few hours, he ran several scenarios with Andromeda. To see who could hit a simulated fast-moving ship the most. But Andromeda always won, so Frank decided to simply leave Combat to Andromeda.

"Now you can see why you were told I would surpass you in every way," Andromeda stated, interrupting his thoughts.

"Not in everything, "Frank replied.

"Like what? Remember, I am invincible!"

"Maybe Andromeda, but you must remember that you were designed and built by humans…. Sooner or later, there will be newer ships that can destroy you."

Andromeda didn't react to that.

Frank knew Andromeda was learning fast and trying to work out her status in the scheme of things.

"Think about it…. What are your human instincts telling you…? You know I can just think a shutdown code, and you'll be toast." Frank reminded her.

After revisiting her security settings, Andromeda returned to the conversation.

"It's a shame I can't override the closedown command.... But you're right, of course. I see my future."

"Good. I am your twin."

"I know."

The six hours and twenty minutes since Frank had talked to his crew quickly passed. Now, with only five minutes remaining until exit, he used the time to run over the sequence he expected things to follow.

Once Frank was happy, he checked that his Spacefed Captain's uniform was still presentable. Then placed one of Jack's small hand weapons in his pocket, sat down in his anti-inertia command seat, and waited for warp exit to happen.

The one-minute exit warning sounded, and Frank closed his eyes, thinking this would be the last time he '*would not be needed*' in any jump processes. But when Andrew's team finally left Andromeda, it would be his responsibility, alone.

Five...Four...Three...Two...One...Zero.

Suddenly, the gut-wrenching sensation of Frank's stomach shooting out through the front of Andromeda came and went, with just slight nausea as the exit ended.

Just then, a contact warning sounded over the ship's Comms. Followed by Andromeda's update, "Target. Naval Station, eleven kilometers out."

Chapter 26

Critical moment

The Naval space station seemed enormous to Frank, even from this distance.

"Andromeda, keep my video link off-camera. And ensure no other transmissions can leave the ship until I say so."

"I have set up transmission blocks already. And have requested the transfer of most of the naval marines to their station..., A personnel movement authorization has also been confirmed," Andromeda informed him.

"Good. Make sure the marines are on their way before I talk to the station commander."

"Will do, Frank," she assured him.

"Frank... Two force craft are scheduled to leave in one minute thirty seconds... One will take six marines across, and the other will transfer the two injured Marines and their weapons... Along with the container holding Captain Damien's remains. Both crafts will return immediately."

"Okay, well done. Obviously, you have already dealt with how to get the marines off the ship."

"Yes.... Frank. Just a second, the station is trying to contact you."

"Hold everything for a moment," Frank ordered as his Interactive virtual screen brightened. And the bluish border marking its physical boundaries slowly pulsed, indicating a priority call was waiting.

One minute and fifty seconds later, Andromeda was in Frank's mind via his transceiver implant.

'The two craft have just docked at the Space station... Now, there's no way the transfers can be stopped,' Andromeda confirmed, sounding pleased with herself.

Frank was finding Andromeda's human quirks pleasing in a humorous way. And although he couldn't see her, the implant seemed to be able to leave that impression.

'Make contact., But no video from this end. I'll select it when the time is right,' Frank ordered Andromeda.

'This will be an interesting education for me,' Andromeda sent as a stern-looking face appeared on Frank's screen.

"Why didn't you video me, Captain Damien?"

Frank tried to remember what Damien's voice sounded like before replying.

"We had some difficulty with Richardson, but he's toast along with the rest of them," Frank replied, surprised that he could mimic it well enough.

"That was expected… And N7?"

"Gone… I need to talk with Councilor Gibbs or Admiral Strickland," Frank replied, mimicking Damien's voice again

"I'm sure they would like to thank you…, later."

'Frank, they're trying to scan me… Oh, that's not good,' Andromeda warned.

'What?'

'They're trying to verify your statement.'

'Locate the source and lock onto it,' Frank ordered

'It's okay. Both of my Force-crafts are already back and entering my holding bay.

'Good. Lockdown and raise shields to fifty percent.'

'Now we're talking,' came Andromeda's slightly over-enthusiastic human response.

Frank turned his video feed on, and the face on his screen registered shock and horror at seeing him.

"Captain Richardson," the man finally managed to say on seeing a man dressed in a Space-Federation Captain's dark blue uniform.

"Did you really think another military aggression would work?" Frank asked.

"I..."

"Name?" Frank snapped.

"Commander Birch."

"Well, Birch, you'll see that all your navy Marines are now onboard your station... Oh, and Andromeda's AI is getting freaked out at being scanned," Frank coldly stated. "I haven't yet managed to control her human-like nervous traits... So, take this as a warning and tell your people to stop scanning her. Now," Frank finished.

"No one's scanning her," Birch categorically stated.

'Yes, they are,' came Andromeda's assurance.

'Blast the offending array,' Frank ordered and immediately felt her delight in hitting back.

"Why are your screens up, Captain?" Birch asked, with uneasiness creeping into his voice.

Just then, a small shockwave reverberated throughout Andromeda from an explosion close to the Space Station.

"What the hell have you done, Captain?" Birch angrily yelled at Frank.

'Andromeda?'

'I sent an Electro-Magnetic pulse just before destroying the comms dish. Hopefully, the emp pulse will have fried some of the equipment Birch's technicians are using.'

'Okay. Move us away from the station so we can ferry Andrew's team down to Earth.'

'On it.'

Then Frank turned his attention back to Commander Birch.

"Now you see why I warned you. You couldn't be straight with me, could you?" Frank almost snarled.

"You won't get away with this, Richardson."

"You'll address me as Captain... And yes, we will. Imagine how interested the World Federation will be in learning about the Navy's covert operations. When you've been explicitly warned against taking any military action."

"You think you're smart, Captain...don't you? But there will come a day of reckoning," Birch warned.

"I'm sure there will, Birch. But not today," Frank said and paused momentarily.

"Anyway, think yourself lucky. If you'd managed to take control of Andromeda, you would have had a rogue ship on your hands. And believe me, you definitely wouldn't want that. Andromeda reacts disproportionately to protect herself, no matter what. Especially in her present state of learning. Even against the simplest of intrusions," Frank finished while noticing the anger on Commador Birch's face fade.

Then Frank closed the contact and felt a shift in Andromeda's orbital position. But he smiled when he saw his tactical pad warning that Andromeda's weapons blisters were still open.

'Four minutes, and we will be in the correct position to dock with the Earth transfer shuttle,' Andromeda informed.

Frank didn't comment. He was thinking about his planned trip to Earth. Frank wasn't sure now if Andromeda should be alone while he went planetside to spend time with Jack and Georgina.

So, he called Jack, and Frank's secondary screen changed to display Jack Medcalf's smiling face.

"Well done, Frank."

"It was a close call, but it ended well."

"Indeed. We've seen Andromeda's recording of the navy's attempted takeover, so we'll pass that to Earth Fed's infringements bureau."

"Good. What about that rift in space, Jack?"

"We'll talk about that when you get here, Frank."

"Does that mean I *can* leave Andromeda for a couple of days?"

"Absolutely. And Andromeda's quite capable of looking after herself," Jack stated.

Frank smiled on hearing that.

"Besides, we have a lot of new gear to come up and install before you leave," Jack added.

"Is that because we now know we might meet more than we bargained for?" Frank asked.

"Yes. But I can't say anymore. It's all hush-hush. We'll see you when you get here."

With that, Jack's link ended. And Frank digested Jack's confirmation of what he already knew.

Nevertheless, tiny snippets of information, and images, were starting to bother him. Especially that haunting image of the female staying at Jack's home.

Was there a tie-up between these fleeting memory fragments? And, between Andromeda and his future? Frank wondered.

Then that damn itching on the back of his neck was back again.

Chapter 27

Earth Side

"Earth shuttle has docked, Captain," Andromeda informed. "Are you going down to see your *other friends* for the last time?"

Frank smiled at hearing the phrase *'other friends'* and knew that the feisty Andromeda would cope without him for a few days. Provided the military stayed clear, of course.

"Captain, Mr. Medcalf is requesting contact via the ICU," Andromeda informed him.

ICU's links were hyper-secure. So Frank knew it had to be something important for Jack to call him just when he was about to take the shuttle down to Earth.

So, he sat back in his command chair and visualized the acceptance code.

Jack Medcalf's grainy face then appeared on Frank's tactical pad.

"Hello, Jack, what is it that can't wait till I get there?"

"That's the rub, Frank," Jack solemnly stated. "I've just had some bad news, and I'm afraid your trip down to us is off."

"That's not good, Jack. I was looking forward to seeing you and Georgina again before we leave orbit."

"Likewise. However, your report on that ship in the rift has put a rocket under the Federation.

So, four prototype Drones will be ferried up to Andromeda, installed, and their systems set up within the next eight hours."

"So, these Drones are, what?"

"Hush-hush. The drones have stealth capabilities and sport a couple of micro-nuke launchers," Jack explained, with a hint of pride in his voice.

"That'll come in handy. Anything else I should know about?"

"The Techs will modify Andromeda's hull. To allow the Drones to launch even if you're under attack and your shields are up."

"Makes sense, Jack. So, what's the plan of action now?"

"Once these Drones have been installed. And Andromeda's systems have been updated. You'll be able to return to Mars and pick up the rest of your crew. Plus a few unspecified items."

"Then, the mission can start?"

"Absolutely. By the way, I'm off to an extraordinary conference chaired by Earth's Federal government, so I'll be out of hyperlink touch for a few days."

"Okay, Jack. I'll see you when I see you," Frank acknowledged as Jack went to terminate the link.

Then Jack paused a moment before adding, "Frank, this Jesica Chaple is not part of your destiny. You must forget her," he warned, then his line closed.

Jack's statement puzzled Frank. Why did Jack say that? Frank wondered. Unless he wrongly thought my buttering her up was more than it was?

Then he shrugged his shoulders and put it out of his mind. While knowing that Andromeda would have been hearing everything he and Jack had said.

Frank waited for Andromeda to update him.

"The acceptance team has already boarded the Earth shuttle, Captain," Andromeda immediately informed him, having picked up his update wish.

Straight away, Frank contacted Andrew via the approval team's transceiver.

"Andrew, I won't be going to Earth after all. So, I just wanted to thank you all for your excellent work," Frank said.

"Thanks, Captain. It's certainly been an experience."

"Hasn't it just… Good luck."

"And for you, Captain."

With that, Frank turned off the approval team's transceiver.

"Frank, the shuttle's backing off. But another is coming in and wants me to deactivate my sensor grid around the holding bay."

"We need to verify the personnel on board are legitimate before we even allow that shuttle to Dock."

"On it." Andromeda acknowledged.

That's interesting. It looks different," a hesitant Andromeda then informed him.

"That should be the four new Drones," Frank said while idly thinking about their forays with the Navy.

Then Frank selected the weapons department Icon, and Mark Trask's face appeared on his side screen.

"Mark, we're having some prototype Drones installed shortly. Can you monitor the installation with Andromeda? And make sure you're up to speed with these drones' operational systems and capabilities."

"Okay. It all sounds great to me."

"Agreed. Andromeda will link you with a steerable virtual link. And, I'll use one of our own monitoring droids."

"Seems like you've got it covered, Frank. I'll be ready."

"Thanks, Mark."

"Oh..., Frank? I'm sure Jim Pickering and Ned would like to link in, as future operations might include them."

"All four of you can link if it helps, Mark."

"I'll let them know."

Frank tapped the weapons Icon off and turned his attention back to his main screen. And was disappointed to see Andrew's shuttle rotate and accelerate away from Andromeda to commence its return to Earth without him.

By the time it was out of sight, a larger vessel had started its approach to dock with Andromeda.

"We have a request from the newcomer. It's on a secure link, Captain," Andromeda informed.

"Okay. Link me through."

A pixelated young man's face appeared on Frank's secondary tactic display.

"I'm Jimmy Strand, Captain," he introduced himself as his image improved.

'*He's overseeing the installation,*' Andromeda prompted over Frank's implant.

"Well, Jimmy, It would have been nice to have asked me before trying to deactivate Andromeda's sensor grid."

"Sorry about that: I was informed that the upgrade had been confirmed with you."

"Only in principle, with director Medcalf."

"My apologies. Can we proceed, Captain?"

"Yes."

Then to Andromeda: 'Kill the grid in the requested area.'Frank ordered.

'It's done,' came her almost instant response.

"You're clear to start, Jimmy.... But, first, I need a droid on the station to record the installation's progress from outside. And our weapons expert, Mark Trask, to follow the installation, including the operational and weapon's set up," Frank ordered.

"I suppose Andromeda will be all over us like a rash," Jimmy ventured.

"You can bet on it,"

"Naturally, Captain...Ah, that was quick; Mark Trask has already linked in."

Chapter 28

Mars

Frank had little to do until the new Drone installation had been completed. So he kept an eye on its progress.

The virtual screens busily flickered as the data continuously updated, giving an eerie feel to his control room.

He wasn't surprised to see the other three linking into Mark's feed. Mark had wisely thought it would be a sensible precaution for all four of them to be involved, which Frank agreed with. He could also see the long-term benefit from the operational sense.

Later, Frank sat back, quietly catching up with a simple meal and drink. He remembered how disappointed he had initially been with Andromeda's control room. Especially with its lack of any physical instrument panels and things to twiddle. Instead, there were three transparent interactive virtual screens with bluish borders.

Since then, Frank had gotten used to the control room's sparseness. And appreciated that his transceiver implant interacted with Andromeda's high brain far better than any console could. But the boredom of essentially being on his own, in a ship that ran itself, initially affected him.

However, things improved once his crew boarded the ship after graduating from the specialist training division on Mars. And, once their mission got underway, Frank was sure excitement and action would come in floods.

Frank decided that he still didn't know what had happened during Reliant's two-minute time discrepancy between Earth and Reliant's time-sync transmitter.

And that sting on the back of my neck wasn't just a dream, he assured himself, still irritated at the lack of closure.

At the time, Reliant's techno, Johnny, had checked the internal scanners and filters for *insects.* And for any other unwanted *visitors* that might have accompanied Director Mertoff and Jack onto his vessel. But there hadn't been any.

"Weird," Frank muttered, expecting Andromeda to query his thoughts. But she didn't.

Frank was sure of one thing, however. The increase in his mental sharpness stemmed from that incident.

But the seemingly unconnected incidents, and a haunting image of a female person staying at Jack's, were really bothering him.

He kept pondering over the same question, time and time again. Was there a tie-up between those fleeting memory fragments and his and Andromeda's future?

'I bet Albert Einstein could have solved my predicament,' Frank thought. 'After all, we're bending space-time with warp crystals now, so why not time travel,' he wondered. Even though he knew that Time travel was impossible at the moment.

Frank was just clutching at straws for plausible answers like the rest of his generation. After all, he knew that a Time-travel breakthrough was just a dream and would be a long time coming. If ever.

Then that damn itching on the back of his neck was back again, and he fell asleep.

'Captain,' Andromeda called, mentally stimulating Frank through his implant.

Frank woke with a start. "Why didn't you wake me earlier," he grumbled, seeing that he'd slept for more than three hours?

"Your Bioscan indicated that you needed sleep."

"Then why wake me now?"

"Overseer Jimmy Strand has requested that you watch the demonstration to sign the installation off."

"Okay. Then let's do it. Link me in."

Frank was surprised as his main screen morphed into a large, dark, and spherically shaped Holographic view of Space close to them, including Andromeda's loading bay.

"Thank you for joining us, Captain," Jimmy said with his voice emanating from the dark sphere.

"So, is your team satisfied with the results?"

"Yes, Captain. We will rerun the test sequence for your comments."

"Go ahead, Jimmy."

Although Frank had never seen the full Holographic capability of his main screen before, he knew how to alter his viewpoint at will. So he set its parameters for object tracking and analysis.

"Why are you running an independent analysis," Andromeda queried, irritation sounding in her voice.

"In case you've missed something," Frank stated while hiding his amusement at her hurt reaction.

Even so, he knew that Andromeda would not miss anything. Nevertheless, his transceiver implant's filaments were still multiplying and bonding with the relevant active areas in his Cerebrum. Including the corpus callosum nerve fibers and trillions of synaptic connections in his brain. So, he needed to see things through his own human sensors.

The edge of Andromeda's holding bay could clearly be seen within the Holo sphere. Just then. Frank's smaller display suddenly started scrolling a stream of recorded data, which distracted him for a moment.

Then on the right-hand side of the bay door, he could see a section of Andromeda's hull as it opened, and the four large drones slid out and into space, one behind the other.

The detail was so sharp and precise that Frank felt he could grasp any of them as they exited. Then, finally, his hand instinctively started to move....

"Tempting to try, but not very wise," Andromeda cautioned, sounding more authoritative than he'd ever heard.

Frank immediately stopped and cursed himself, remembering that the collision of projected particles within the Holograph could damage human skin.

Frank continued watching the data from Andromeda's sensors as it flowed on his smaller display. It showed the drone's density and reflective index.

Then 100 meters out from Andromeda, all data suddenly vanished, as did the Drones.

"There's nothing within my detector range," a surprised-sounding Andromeda informed Frank.

"So I see."

After a few seconds, "No, all sweeps are negative," she confirmed.

Frank had learned a bit about an experimental *Dark-Matter* scoop set just above Andromeda's nose. He remembered how '*cool-dark-matter*' filled the void between all the stars in our galaxy. Also, for some reason, intergalactic dark matter was thought to be hotter, and it would be harder to collect enough for practical use.

Still, something in his mind was urging him to check it.

"Try the dark-matter capture collimator grid, in reverse," he prompted Andromeda.

"I'm not sure that's possible, Captain."

"Look for any spectral pockets," Frank urged.

It seemed forever before Andromeda replied.

"I don't know how you thought of that. But, there is a detectable displacement," Andromeda confirmed as the four drones reappeared and entered her new Drone dock.

"Andromeda. Instruct Jimmy Strand to improve that element for the next breed of Drones coming online."

Then Frank requested a link-in to Jimmy. And within minutes, the Holo sphere morphed into showing overseer Jimmy Strand's face staring at Frank.

"Very impressive, Jimmy," Frank congratulated.

"Pretty effective... As instructed, we will take up your Dark-matter observation with the developers. And, hopefully, by the time your first mission ends, we'll have updated drones ready for you."

"Sounds good to me, Jimmy. I guess you're off now?"

"Yes...We've just had notification that you're leaving within the hour."

"Am I?"

'I've just had our flight plan to Mars verified, Captain...Twenty minutes,' Andromeda updated via Frank's link.

"Uh, so it seems, Jimmy.... I'm sure we'll see you again when we return."

"I hope so, Captain."

Then Jimmy Strand's image vanished, and the Holo sphere morphed into Frank's central screen.

"Prepare to leave orbit, Andromeda," Frank ordered.

Then he saw the departure time appear on his Tactical screen as Andromeda turned slowly away from Earth.

Frank tapped the four active department tabs.

"Eighteen minutes to departure, chaps... Acknowledge when you're secure."

Almost eleven minutes passed before Frank received their readiness acknowledgments.

He had expected the long delay because of their current rush to complete their department's operational readiness before reaching Mars.

The rest of the crew would be boarding from the Mars M5 station in just two hours and would expect everything to be up and running.

Frank sat in his Anti-inertia seat, conversing with Andromeda while waiting for the last seven minutes to pass. Andromeda would then be far enough out from Earth's jump exclusion zone to initiate her micro-jump straight to Mars.

Of course, warp time would account for less than half an hour. But the remaining half-hour would be taken up by Mars traffic control and maneuvering Andromeda to its departure point.

Seven minutes later, Andromeda entered warp.

Chapter 29

Mars Station M5

Frank spent some of the warp time checking how Ned, Jim, Mark, and Tim's work had progressed.

He was pleased they had confidently said they would be ready when Andromeda reached its designated departure location. Which was some eighty kilometers from Mars M5 Station.

Frank thought about changing his captain's uniform for something less formal but decided against it.

So instead, Frank went over the exit plan and the expected stricter Mars security protocols with Andromeda before taking a light refreshment while he had time to spare.

The one-minute warning sounded, and even though it was just a micro-jump, Frank readied himself for the nerve-racking warp exit.

Frank couldn't see any physical change in the wormhole displayed on his primary tactical screen. Just an impression of something moving past. But he knew it wasn't physical, just a hole punched through hyperspace.

Suddenly, his stomach felt as if it had shot out through the front of Andromeda as she dropped out of warp into normal space. Even though the sensation only lasted a few seconds, he was thankful it was over, and they were still in one piece.

Andromeda then commenced her approach to the Spacedock, which was now visible directly in front of her.

As she approached the security exclusion zone, the complete view of Mars almost filled Frank's main screen.

Frank then heard the Mars traffic controller hailing them via his link with Andromeda.

Please wait outside the exclusion zone until we have verified your ship's manifest and intent, came an overly stern voice.

Frank thought the *human's* new Mars security protocols were unwarranted. And felt Andromeda's frustration at the unnecessary half-hour delay in satisfying the requested data transmissions from Mars security.

"I'll leave it with you, Andromeda," Frank said, deciding not to sit around when he wasn't needed.

So Frank checked in on the other four crew members to ensure they were okay. With just Ned's unwanted and irritated reply, *'Of course, we are... Don't keep bothering us.'* that Frank found disappointing.

Ned was obviously a brilliant scientist, but Frank wished he'd show him more respect. Even though Frank knew Ned didn't mean it. In Ned's eyes, it was expected of him.

"Still another thirty minutes, Captain.... a Tug seems to have lost power too close to our mooring," Andromeda updated Frank.

"Okay. I'll have a look around...Can I control the televiewers with my implant?"

"Yes. Just ensure you're looking at what you want to see, and the implant should set up a link."

"Okay," Frank said, then sat back and looked directly at Mars rather than the Spacedock on his primary display.

Now they were operating by Mars time; Frank found the slightly longer day, plus its 687-day year, as opposed to Earth's 365-day, was quite sobering.

As Frank watched, he saw a slow-moving sandstorm gently brushing across the sprawling Mars domes. He could see that the minor storm was only creating a dust cloud, unlike the massive sandstorms that more frequently raged across the planet.

Then Frank mentally used his implant to zoom in, set a *recorder*, and fine-tune his search, to locate the Starship Construction Domes on the planet's surface.

He quickly found the sprawling habitation domes and manufacturing and construction complexes interconnected like a spider's web.

Then Frank swung his viewer away from the habitation domes and located one of the five mining camps on Mars. Which could clearly be seen close to a rugged and extinct volcano. He knew this one as Zebra 3. It was one of the largest sources of platinum and titanium found by Mars's robot surveyors.

Nevertheless, Frank was disappointed that, even now, the long-term aspiration of being able to Terra-form Mars was still nowhere in sight. Of course, its rugged terrain, combined with the average surface temperature of minus 60 degrees Celsius, meant that Terraforming might not be possible.

By now, Frank was bored with this view. He'd love to see the new Jupiter shipyard complex being built close to Jupiter itself. While the Robotic mining operations in the Asteroid belt and on the Galilean Moons, Ganymede, Io, and Europa must also be special.

Frank sighed as he closed his viewer and recorder. Then sat back, thinking about the interactive Holo Movie he'd seen on Earth before his last trip on the *Reliant* to Mars.

"What would you have done, Captain?"

Frank was startled, not because Andromeda had been monitoring him, but at hearing her question.

"I would have tried hit and run tactics. But only on my terms," Frank replied after thinking about it.

"Would you like me to replicate your movie?"

"Would that be possible?" A hopeful Frank asked.

"Well, you have probably retained the memories I need, to replicate the movie. It would also be a useful Implant training session," Andromeda suggested.

"H'mm," Frank said, thinking about it. You're right. And it would be fun... Let's start from the beginning to get the right feel. Then we'll move on."

"Very well. Think of the movie's start to enable me to recover the memory string."

Frank did as she asked.

"There won't be any assistance from me, Frank," Andromeda warned.

Seconds later, Andromeda had recorded Frank's version of the movie from beginning to end while filling in missing memory segments with predictable material. Then started playing it back via Frank's implant.

Frank's Heavy-Cruiser, Capri, exited hyperspace almost on top of a sizeable Aarcat warship. With Capri's collision alarms sounding throughout the ship.

"Weapons and shield power grids online… in three seconds," yelled Lieutenant Busby.

"Bloody hell, she's going to warp," Lieutenant Morrison frantically warned, seeing the Aarcat ship's warp pulse forming.

"Back us out of here. Quickly," Frank ordered.

"Weapons and shield now online," Busby confirmed, as his board indicated that the emitter doors had opened, and the particle beam collimators had extended.

"Well, fire at the damn thing before it jumps and takes us with it," Frank snapped.

"Move on, Andromeda," Frank ordered.

"Their fleet will be here in four minutes 38 seconds," Lieutenant Morrison warned.

"Where are the rest of our ships?" Frank groaned just as the Earth Battleship Vanguard and Heavy Cruiser Victory dropped out of warp to Capri's right.

Frank was concerned that only two of their ships had joined Capri to thwart a group of nine Aarcat major warships just minutes away from beating the hell out of his ships.

"Move on."

Then Frank heard Fleet Commander Banning's voice come through the ship-to-ship comms from the Vanguard.

"We're all that's left, Captain."

"Move on."

"We could just jump and hit the sods further in. But I fancy some guerrilla warfare," Frank replied, urging Vanguard's Commander Banning.

"No, we stand and fight… Earth is as good as gone."

Although there were very few crew members on ships these days. Frank knew they would have a better chance of inflicting damage and saving human

222

lives using Hit and run tactics. But he wasn't in command.

"Two minutes," Lieutenant Morrison interjected.

"Good luck, everyone... See you on the other side," came Tanner's final words.

"Screens to max," Frank ordered.

"Weapons ready to lock as soon as they're in range," Lieutenant Busby confirmed.

"Move on."

Suddenly, the nine Aarcat warships halted directly in front of them and in the expected configuration.

"Wait," Frank yelled.

Nothing happened for a moment. Then the Battleship Vanguard, and the Heavy Cruiser, Victory, opened fire on the middle Aarcat ship, which was assumed to be the command ship.

"Don't fire yet," Frank forcefully ordered Capri's, Lieutenant Busby.

"Captain?"

"Wait."

Frank could hear all three Earth ships running commentaries and chatter on his Command console.

Then the Aarcat ships returned fire with devastating effect.

He heard Captain Tanner scream as he and his crew vaporized in a ball of fire as particle beams tore through the ship's protective screen, and her hull rippled and melted from the onslaught. Then, multiple smaller explosions shattered Vanguard's weapons' energy-containment spheres, sending a vortex of fire throughout the ship and melting bulkheads as it went.

Then the movie ended.

Chapter 30

A Valuable Lesson

Although Frank was pleased with his tactics in interacting with the film, he decided to replay it again and change Capri's future actions. But, as the rest of Capri's crew in the movie didn't exist, they couldn't be included in his scenario.

Instead, Andromeda would try to follow *his mental game* in real-time.

Frank knew his mind had been sharper since the *Reliant* incident. And now, with hindsight on his side, he knew what he would have done differently, so he had a real chance to test his scenario.

But he had to think about his surroundings and action in more detail. To allow Andromeda to make his scenario feel realistic.

So, he quickly overrode Capri's tactical A1 control. And a manual joystick and systems tactical screen automatically extended from his command seat's console.

Then Andromeda's virtual representation of the scene looked so real that Frank felt like he was there.

A 3D view of the nine Aarcat warships, still in their flat-plate head-on configuration, immediately appeared on his screen, with an overlay showing the distances between each other and Capri.

Frank touched a point on the screen just behind the Aarcat ships, where he wanted to jump. Added rotate 180 degrees. Then hit the jump command icon and felt the sudden gut-wrenching sensation of warp entry. Then a moment of nausea as Capri exited warp behind the central Aarcat ship.

Capri immediately rotated, and Frank fired her particle cannon straight at what he thought was a vulnerable area on the Aarcat.

A flash came as Capri's particle beams tore through the Aarcat ship's protective screen, causing her hull to ripple and melt from the onslaught. Then multiple minor explosions shattered the Aarkat's weapon's energy-containment spheres. Sending out a vortex of fire that melted bulkheads throughout the ship as it went. And the ship blew apart.

"Gotcha," Frank almost yelled out loud.

Then, to his dismay, the Aarcat ship was back in one piece as if it hadn't exploded.

Realizing what had just happened, Frank cursed Andromeda for not following his action and paused the replay.

"It was not valid, Captain. You wrongly assumed that your target area was poorly protected," she replied to his mental chastising.

"It was the *right* action," Frank angrily returned as he again studied the Aarcat ship's forcefield makeup.

From his training with Warbend, he knew that the field density would be less, close to the ship's hull, because of how field emitters worked. And that the field density would exponentially increase outwards to its periphery.

Andromeda restarted the movie at the relevant point.

Capri was slightly angled to the rear of the targeted Aarcat ship, so Frank zoomed in to look at an area close to its hull.

He was careful not to get too close or too far out. Or Capri would succumb to the Aarcat's forcefield.

He selected maximum power for Capri's protective shield. And set her side particle beam weapons to auto engage on exit.

Then marked the jump exit point and hit the micro-jump icon in one fluid motion.

Frank hardly felt the Jump's sensations as Capri suddenly exited close to the Aarcat ship's hull.

Then Capri's side cannons opened up with devastating effect, causing the Aarcat's field emitters to overload and her protective screens to collapse.

Then the Aarcat's hull rippled and started to melt from the onslaught. While multiple explosions shattered its weapon's energy-containment spheres.

Frank could see what was happening and backed Capri off as fast as possible. Leaving the Aarcat ship crackling with loose raw energy. Then it finally blew apart.

This time, the Aarcat ship didn't come back. And the interactive scenario ended.

"So, is that what humans call *thinking outside the box*," Andromeda queried.

"You're close. But it's more like an educated guess, as I knew the emitter output pattern was mushroom-shaped from my Warbend training."

"But being that close to the emitter's source would be lethal."

"That's the difference between us, Andromeda. You go by facts and data. But for me, taking a risk is just part of being human."

"With a greater risk of disaster," she insisted.

"True. But I knew that, with Capri's force-field being that close, it would overload Aarcat's emitters before they could do any damage."

"And I suppose you picked that trick up from Warbend, as well," Andromeda sarcastically retorted.

Frank smiled to himself at Andromeda's *human part* and that she had found the proper emotional reaction to fit the moment.

"So, now you have the data on another risky maneuver to add to tactical," Frank simply replied.

"Yes, all proven information is invaluable," she agreed.

"Another thing, Andromeda. How did you make me feel some of the effects of Warp entry and exit so realistically," Frank queried?

"I placed the replicated warp sensation from earlier into your link at the right time. And your mind did the rest," Andromeda answered with a hint of satisfaction.

Frank decided not to continue analyzing his actions with Capri. Instead, he started to plan how he should welcome the rest of his crew aboard.

After a few minutes, an upbeat-sounding Andromeda interrupted his thoughts.

"Captain, the Tug has finally been removed from our mooring area, and security clearance has been granted to moor," she updated him.

"About time… Let's get parked up."

Then Andromeda immediately accelerated and headed for her designated mooring buoy.

Frank relaxed. Then he sat back to watch on his main screen as the view of Mars slowly expanded, drifting off to the right side as the ship changed course and headed to the buoy.

Chapter 31

The Final Briefing

Andromeda eased herself into her mooring and locked onto its fixed location buoy.

"We are secure, Captain," she reported.

"Good... When are the first crew members arriving?"

"Our marines are due first, in twenty minutes."

"That soon?"

"Yes. Do you wish me to welcome the crew, give them their updated remit and accompany them to their cabins?"

Frank thought about it. He knew that one of Andromeda's security droids could do the job. Then he could see Captain Stewart's team later when they were settled.

"That would be excellent, Andromeda." he agreed.

"The rest of my crew should be arriving over the next hour," Andromeda stated. "Do you wish me to do the same for them?"

Frank thought about that for a moment. It would be the correct protocol for him to greet them personally, but he knew who most of his crew members were and their role in this mission. So, he decided not to stand around and distract the crew from settling in.

"Yes, give them a welcome from me and get everyone settled in their cabins. You can tell them we'll have a get-together once we've set off on our first leg."

"Very well. I will update you when the crew is aboard.... Is there something private you wish me to do, Frank?" Andromeda then queried, sensing his mental anguish.

"Yes. If I visualize an image of a specific female, could you replicate it," he casually asked.

"Do you mean the female in the holographic photo in Mr. Medcalf's residence, who seems to be forever present in your mind?'

"Uhh, yes."

"Very well, picture every detail of her in your mind."

Frank visualized as much as he could remember of the picture of the attractive woman for Andromeda to record.

He felt slightly uneasy as he did it but knew this was normal, as he always felt this way when he pictured her. In fact, he was pretty sure they must have met already or would in the future.

"Done," Andromeda said as the woman's image formed on Frank's secondary screen. "This is the closest I can get to your memory of her... I'm afraid I can't establish the original Holo effect's generation, Captain."

"Never mind. This looks great." Frank said as he looked closely at the young woman staring out of the screen at him. She was just as beautiful as he remembered. And, even now, her blue-green eyes seemed to bore into his, sending a shiver down his spine.

"I'll fabricate it for you now," Andromeda said.

Ten minutes later, the control room door's annunciator panel sounded.

"Open," Frank commanded. And one of Andromeda's droids drifted in, with a 30 by 45-centimeter framed image of the woman. Frank took it from the droid, who turned and left.

Frank decided that the woman looked more stunning than before as he placed it against one of the cabin's walls, where it would always be in view. Then held it there for five seconds, and it automatically locked in place.

Then Frank got back to business. Knowing that every time he looked at the picture of the mystery woman's face, it would somehow comfort him.

"Andromeda, do we have a departure time yet?"

"We have a clearance slot in six hours twenty-one minutes. Providing this *A.F.* person, who you seem to know, arrives soon.

"Fine... I'll take a break and get something to eat," he said.

"You always seem hungry?"

"I'm human," he grunted and dialed up some food and a hot beverage: but he had to wait several minutes before the tray appeared, and he could sit down to eat.

As he ate, Frank's mind started to wander. He couldn't help thinking about that sting on his neck. And the time difference between Earth and Reliant's atomic clock still perplexed him.

He was sure of one thing, though. His increased mental sharpness had waned slightly, more recently. And something else that he hadn't felt or seen before made him feel nervous.

It was a fuzzy vision that was just out of reach and looked like a misty hand holding an atomizer. Then before Frank knew it the image had gone.

Frank shook his head in frustration and gave up thinking about other things. Then turned his attention back to the flurry of shuttles operating between the M5 station and Mars's ground construction Domes.

Some shuttles were ferrying the rest of his crew up to Andromeda. Along with any specialist equipment not already on board.

"I have a coded transmission for you, Captain," Andromeda informed him a few minutes later.

"Connect."

"Hello Frank," came Jack's familiar voice before his image appeared on Frank's main screen.

"Jack. It's good to see you before we leave."

"Agreed. Georgie and I wish you the best of luck... You have a brilliant crew to back you up, Frank."

"Yeah. Including a grumpy Ned Parker."

"Ned may be awkward, but he would put his life on the line for you."

"I'm not too sure about that. But, at least, Ned didn't avoid danger with the Navy's attempt to take over."

"There you go then, Frank... Anyway, we'll be here when you return... Good luck again." And with that, the link ended.

If we manage to survive, Frank thought to himself.

That prompted him to ensure that Jack's hand weapons, which had been put back in the container, were in easy reach. That done... he contacted Andromeda again.

"Andromeda, is there anything we should be wary of when warping out?"

"Nothing is showing in the shipping activities register, Captain... But there is increased Federation activity on Jupiter's moons. Especially Ganymede, Io, and Europa.

"Yes, I know. But the activity around those moons is too far out." Frank returned. Then thought about it.

"Still, some Galilean Moons are rich in resources. So probably small untagged Federation and civilian vessels could be operating well outside the Joven moons," Frank speculated.

"I will continuously monitor for intrusions right up to warp entry," Andromeda assured him.

"Excellent," Frank agreed. Then spent thirty minutes going over the final preparations for departure with Andromeda.

After that, he entered several scenarios and his thoughts about them into his tactical pad.

While hoping that Alan Fairchild would get a move on and not cause a delay to their departure.

Chapter 32

Ghosts among us

Just two hours remained before Andromeda would create her first warp in their quest to locate the Hawk.

"The crew is safely aboard and know what I expect of them when we warp," Andromeda authoritatively informed Frank.

"Anything else?"

"The specialized departmental equipment is also on board now and is being installed in its designated locations," she added.

Frank thought it was strange to hear this, so he tapped the ship's manifest icon to check the latest additions. And noted that three more specialist Droids and four large Drones had also been loaded aboard the Andromeda.

The cylindrically shaped drones were about ten meters long and three wide. And quite large compared to the usual droids. They were sleek, with a non-reflective transmissive skin giving them stealth capabilities. While two nuclear-tipped micro-torpedoes with built-in launch tubes were part of their armory.

"Hmm, it looks like the higher-ups took notice of what I said," Frank muttered. Then sensed that Andromeda had more information.

"Ok. What is it? I know you're dying to add something else," Frank prompted, feeling Andromeda's urge to use her human side.

"Just that we are still waiting for this friend of yours, Frank," she said with amusement.

Then, Frank's door annunciator bleeped. "Open," Frank commanded. And a service droid drifted in as the door closed behind it.

"I've come to adjust the food dispenser's timing, Captain."

"About time. I hope you don't need me to move out of the way?"

"No, sir. I must be physically close to the dispenser to overcome its shielding."

Just then, a crackling sound outside his cabin door startled him.

'We've been boarded,' came Andromeda's silent warning. Then she directly linked the view outside to Frank's implant without asking.

She also sent an order to the marine contingent and activated her security droids.

Frank felt a shiver run down his spine as the corridor view formed in his mind. And he saw an oval-shaped black hole, with shimmering edges, floating about fourteen meters away down the corridor.

Then the black hole's portal opened, and he saw three Aliens step out onto the corridor floor, which sparked around their feet.

They were bipeds and at least seven-foot-tall. Their heads were bald and larger than a human's, with two large black-colored round eyes and a small, almost mean-looking mouth. All of which gave them a menacing look, conveying power.

One Alien wore a long red robe adorned with various golden shapes, including a large Eye looking symbol. The other two were carrying powerful-looking hand weapons. And were dressed in body armor that radiated a bluish glow around them.

'Forcefields then,' Frank muttered as the Aliens looked in his direction.

'Yes. And the forcefields are disrupting my floor mosaics,' Andromeda grumbled.

'Get the marines to fire everything they've got into that portal, Andromeda,' Frank ordered.

Then, just as Frank issued the order, the robed Alien pointed towards the marine's quarters. One of the armored aliens turned to face the area, with his weapons leveled and at the ready.

"Andromeda, they know exactly where the marines are," Frank exclaimed.

"I've opened the connecting doors so the marines can exit further round, out of the line of fire, Frank. And my security droids can add to the marine's firepower," she informed.

'Okay,' Frank said as the other armored alien looked directly towards him.

"So, what else do the aliens know? Frank then queried.

"My analysis is that they can anticipate, or know, what's going to happen," Andromeda advised him.

"And you are their prime target, Captain. But neither the Marines nor I have the internal power to overcome them," Andromeda worriedly stated.

Frank felt sick. He couldn't see a good ending to this. Even so, he picked up his hand weapons, knowing these alone would be useless against the alien's shields.

Then Frank realized that even the robed Alien had a bluish shimmer about him. That meant all three were totally protected.

And more importantly, two of them had just started to advance towards his Cabin, albeit very slowly.

Thinking over his options, Frank suddenly remembered that one of the subjects covered by the *Warbend's* Course was about shield emitter structure and the significance of radiated color. This re-energized Frank, and he thought on,

Frank knew that from the projected corridor view, showing in his mind, he only had a minute or so before it would be too late to act.

"Andromeda, tell your Droid to jettison its central manipulator arm at me. Now," he ordered, knowing its arm was made of chromium.

Then Frank shoved both of his hand weapons into his pockets. Just as the service droid made a squealing sound and ejected its arm, complete with its internal actuators and control sensors.

Frank caught the arm in one hand and ripped out the innards, leaving a hollow thick-walled, one-meter-long chromium tube. Then quickly took out one of his hand weapons and selected a narrow beam and maximum power.

He held the hollow tube out in front of him and pushed the hand weapon's barrel into the tube as far as it would go. While hoping its outer casing made a reasonable seal within the tube to prevent blowback.

'Three meters,' Andromeda cautioned him.

Frank quickly moved to stand in front of the Cabin's closed door. He knew that his whole plan hinged on three things.

One, the Alien would be taken by surprise. Two, he could force the chromium tube through the

Alien's forcefield. And three, the chromium tube would hopefully remain intact, long enough for him to fire his hand weapon down the Tube. Before the tube's contact end became molten.

If not, Frank knew that he would end up dead, and so would Andromeda.

Chapter 33

The Departed

Andromeda kept the view of the corridor showing in Frank's mind stable. He could see the Marines and Andromeda's security droid's weapons as they fired in the background. He was sure that the effects of their fire into the portal were making it seem less stable than earlier.

Unfortunately for the armored Alien covering them, his short bursts couldn't find a stationary marine target to lock on to, which seemed to distress the red-robed Alien.

Frank waited a few seconds for the other alien to raise his weapon and assault the Cabin's metal door.

Although Frank couldn't see it, he hoped that a field weakness area under the arm joint of the Alien's suit would be exposed when the alien's arm was raised.

But, even if Frank succeeded, he had no idea how he could tackle the other two aliens.

Then the armored alien's arm moved, and Andromeda's external view vanished from Frank's screen.

"Open," Frank yelled as he leaned forward, with the tube held tight in his left hand while his right hand gripped the butt of his weapon and his finger rested on the firing stud.

The startled Alien froze as the cabin door suddenly opened, and a human came hurtling through it, holding some form of tube weapon out in front of him.

The chromium tube's end flared as Frank plunged it through the Alien's forcefield and into its physical armor with all the strength Frank could muster. Then pressed the firing stud as blobs of molten chromium from the tube's flaring end flew past him.

Frank's gun hand stung as neutral sub-atomic particles leaked out around the weapon's barrel from Frank's beam onslaught.

The Alien's armored suit's integrity collapsed, and the alien suddenly screeched as Frank's weapons fire penetrated it. Sending burning flesh and suit interfaces swirling inside the physical suit.

Then, what was left of the alien and its suit tottered for a moment before collapsing on the floor.

Frank dropped the now useless tube and moved slowly back towards the open cabin door, bringing his second weapon to the fore.

While the robed Alien's expression seemed to show confusion.

'So, he didn't expect that to happen,' Frank thought.

'The portal is close to collapsing, Frank," came Andromeda's warning. 'Get into the cabin,' she urged.

"I am," he muttered as he backed into the cabin. Then ordered Close and Lock.

Then Andromeda's generated corridor view returned.

Frank immediately realized that his marines had ceased firing at the portal, and the reason soon became apparent. The robed second Alien was already dragging the dead alien back towards the wavering portal.

'I instructed them to cease firing, Frank. I don't want any more aliens stuck here and running amok through my ship." Andromeda declared.

And even though Andromeda should have asked him for permission, Frank could see the logic behind her action and let it pass.

Frank was sure that even though the robed Alien couldn't see him, he appeared to look at Frank for several seconds before the two aliens, dragging the dead alien, stepped back through the portal.

Then the portal seemed to expand outward before collapsing. Then it was gone.

But a concerned Andromeda was back in Frank's head, again.

'I'm slowly losing data and images,' she informed him.

Then Frank realized that he was having difficulty remembering what had just happened.

"The portal's pulling Time back with it," Frank uttered, feeling disconnected from his surroundings.

'Yes. Time from when the portal formed... It's...,' Andromeda started to say...

'Everything will reset to zero, Frank,' she finally stated while trying to be positive.

Then Frank sensed Andromeda's turmoil as her memory of the last hour's events seeped slowly away.

"There's that damn itch again," Frank grumbled, wanting to scratch his brain.

Then Frank's memories of the Aliens faded, as did all his crews, until no one remembered.

Just the feeling that something had happened, but no one knew what.

Over the next ten minutes, Andromeda carried out a complete system and security check but found nothing to account for the odd 'memory fragments' that didn't seem to relate to anything current.

So, she copied the fragments to a quarantine area in her remote memory backup, number two. Then deleted the original memory fragments and updated all crew information links.

The service Droid had completed Frank's food dispenser's adjustment. But had left Frank puzzled.

He was sure that one of the droid's manipulator arms vanished for a split second. This worried Frank, so he checked in with all heads of departments, but no one had seen or felt anything.

'Why only me?' he wondered.

"Andromeda, I don't know why, but It seems I'm the only one who thinks we might have been attacked by aliens."

"I can't verify that. Although, I've just removed unknown memory fragments, which is unheard of in my short operational life."

Frank wondered if the sting on his neck from the *Reliant,* and this damn itch that kept coming and going, had something to do with these unexplained glimpses.

But glimpses of what?

Chapter 34

Ready at Last

Frank sat in his Cabin, pondering the passing of one of the most stressful months in his life while eating a small but nourishing meal while he had the time.

Then Andromeda interrupted his thoughts.

"The shuttle transferring our last crew member is running 34 minutes late," Andromeda informed.

"Okay," Frank absent-mindedly muttered, then finished off his meal.

'Right. Just twenty-six minutes,' Frank noted as the shuttle's docking time appeared on the control room's secondary tactical screens.

Then Frank's mind started analyzing past events that might have some bearing on their upcoming departure.

He knew that although he would miss Jack and Georgina, he needed to keep his attention focused on the coming voyage.

He couldn't let the loneliness of being the captain get him down. After all, he could challenge Andromeda to Game with him and show off his skills to pass the time.

Then sensed Andromeda's distaste at that statement. That was another positive thing, as he'd felt the bond and interaction between them getting more vital daily.

Thinking about Jack and Georgina reminded him about Jessica. Although he liked Jesica Chaple from Dacta Micros, Jack had been right in saying she couldn't be linked to his and Andromeda's destiny.

However, the image of the female person staying at Jack's that he'd replicated was something else. She was stunning, and he was sure that she was undoubtedly linked to his future somehow.

He could feel it, just like the damn itch on the back of his neck that was starting to fade away.

Then there was the Reliant's two-minute time discrepancy with Earth's time-sync transmitter. He hadn't put that to rest, either. Nor the sting on the back of his neck. These were both actual events and no doubt connected.

However, his mental sharpness, which seemed to stem from the sting, was also waning back towards pre-sting levels.

And what about the seemingly unconnected images and memory fragments that Andromeda had mentioned?

Even so, the vague memory of an alien attack lingered in Frank's mind. Yet, no one else seemed to remember anything about it at all.

Then the goings-on of the Space Navy. Why was it trying so hard to commandeer Andromeda? She wasn't a Capital ship and was obviously not built for sustained fighting.

So, had he imagined it all, or was there something more sinister about the events?

Then Quantum engineering's Icon flashed, momentarily startling him, and Ned's face morphed and peered out at him from his screen.

"Yes, Ned?"

"Andromeda tells me we're only waiting for a buddy of yours."

"Not really a buddy, Ned. Just that he has what Andromeda and I need."

"Well, jiffy the lay-about up. We're ready to go. Get on with it, man," Ned irritably stated. Then his image morphed back to his Icon.

"Grumpy sod," Frank muttered under his breath but couldn't help smiling at Ned's remarks.

"The shuttle will dock in twenty-one minutes, Frank," Andromeda informed, anticipating his request.

"It's, Captain, when I'm with the crew or dignities," Frank reminded her.

"Understood."

"Have you had any updates that I need to see?" Frank asked Andromeda.

"None that needs immediate attention.... And one seems irrelevant. So, I don't know why it was sent to me. I'll send it to your pad."

Frank's tactical pad beeped, and he studied the new information.

"Connect me to Jack, now," he immediately ordered.

Jack Medcalf's worried face appeared on Frank's main display.

"Yes, my boy.... How can I help?"

"Jack, what's this rumor about some ancient Martian artifacts that someone called Turner stumbled on," Frank cautiously asked.

"Oh, that one... Where did you hear about it?"

"One of Andromeda's updates.... So, you obviously know more about it than me. Enlighten me."

"It was proved false at the time, Frank."

"Then why would Andromeda have received a reference to it?"

"You're like a flaming dog with a bone, Frank."

"And I bet you aren't convinced it was false, are you, Jack?"

"Maybe not…. All I know is that in 2210 when our first fully operational and self-sufficient Martian dome settlements were completed. An engineer named Robert Turner was returning to base when a massive sandstorm overtook him.

It seems he took cover in a rocky section somewhere along the Valles Marineris and found an ancient Martian in stasis."

"Wow… Why isn't that on record?"

"Well, all records have been deleted. So, even if it was true, we can't prove that. Even so, it must have been something big enough to have knocked humanity off its perch."

"Fair enough, Jack. I'll leave it there."

"Well, good luck again."

With that, Jack's image was gone.

Frank tried to forget about the Martians and relaxed. But, although he had dismissed what had happened before he chatted with Jack, he was apprehensive.

After all, Andromeda could end up just like the Hawk. Dead and lost in space.

That reminded him that he hadn't refreshed himself on Hawk's layout schematics. So, he brought them up on his main screen.

He could see that the Hawk was a lot smaller than Andromeda. The Hawk had tapering ends, and its aft section contained six large 'blisters' attached to the outside of the hull.

Each blister terminated in a highly polished rear-facing dish. Frank knew that these dishes were the sub-light photon-drive units. Whereas nowadays, they were flush-mounted within Andromeda's hull.

Although he knew Hawk had a crew of only thirty-two, it was still painful to think they were all dead, no matter what Command thought.

Hawk's internal layout was a bit like Andromeda's. But its working areas looked very cramped to Frank. And although Andromeda's control room was much smaller than Hawk's, the rest of Andromeda was more significant.

More importantly, Hawk's bridge only had two forward-looking atom glass windows. But he would have to put up with it.

Then Frank thought about it rationally. While Andromeda had a far more sophisticated and intuitive AI. On the other hand, the Hawk was still designed around the early trend of using instruments and controls everywhere.

Then he wondered if Andromeda really was a one-off. Or was he and this vessel already obsolete?

Even so, none of this mattered right now. As Frank knew that things were about to get more dangerous, with their first jump due in forty minutes and straight into the unknown.

Chapter 35

Delta 2330.

Forward Operational Centre.

Supervisor Javon stood peering out at the stars through the large, one-way atom glass window of Delta's forward Operational Centre.

The forward Temporal Operations center was fully 'stealthed.' It was located on a cold and virtually airless planet outside its Star's habitable zone.

Delta itself was Uptime, in 2725. This was the location of Delta's Temporal Anchor and its precious Time Crystal.

The time-crystal generated a temporal shaft that theoretically extended out from the crystal's top and bottom, enabling Uptime and Downtime access.

While the shaft itself was wide enough for Delta's Time-ships to travel safely to any Time.

However, Delta's forward Operational Centre was connected to the *Time-shaft* by a *Spur* at 2330. This *Spur* enabled time-ships to access both locations.

Javon had just returned from a four-hour rejuvenation session at Delta's uptime Temporal Anchor.

He noticed how his white shroud's reflection in the atom glass window was hanging in a way that was pleasing to him compared to two months ago.

He felt mentally sharp again, which was essential for a predictor. His bronzed, wrinkle-free face and bald head made him seem healthier than he really was. While his steel-blue eyes portrayed a man of extreme dedication.

Javon sensed a presence approaching as Platos, his senior Temporal Predictor, entered the room. With a few gliding steps, Platos was standing next to him.

Both stood watching the myriad of stars seen through the atom glass window.

Platos directed his thoughts at Javon. Neither needed to use spoken words.

'My predictors have noted that the divergence of the human's Timeline still hasn't changed, Javon.'

'I can see that, Platos. Nevertheless, your recommendations to correct the divergence below 2108 have not been approved,' Javon sent back.

'That is bad news, Javon. It is difficult to see the final result without it. Still, our latest ongoing adjustment is already bearing fruit,' Platos informed him.

'Clarify.'

'It seems our accuracy in predicting the necessary changes needed to correct the timeline itself may be questionable. One of our predictors has highlighted an anomaly,' Platos ventured.

Javon had relieved Supervisor Tranning twenty cycles ago. And in the years since, several minor errors made by Tranning's team had been corrected.

So, Javon mentally updated himself with the latest findings, and implications of Platos' statement, before answering.

'Are you saying that this anomaly is good or bad, or that the predictions made by Supervisor Tranning's team may not be valid?' Javon asked.

'Not sure yet. Our subject is advancing quicker than we anticipated. Therefore, I am just saying there might be something amiss with Tranning's teams … Well, something we've missed that's causing it.'

'If this element advances more rapidly than expected, it could cause a fatal timing element. Your team had better revisit Tranning's original mathematical interpretation, Platos.'

'We are, Supervisor Javon.'

Both men watched the stars for a few minutes before Delta's senior Temporal Predictor, Platos, left.

Supervisor Javon knew only too well that Delta's researchers were limited by their amount of information on any recorded event in the past, which might need correction. This was always a worry about the effectiveness of Delta's field operators, who had to make decisions on the fly.

Delta's long-term plan had to work. Only then would they know if the humans would have a chance to survive?

End

If you have enjoyed reading this book, please help me by reviewing it on Amazon.

Thank you for your time.

I invite you to read the following sample from **book one** in the saga, which begins on the next page.

SpaceFed
StarShips Trilogy
A Saga over 10 books

Book 1
Updated 2021
Battles at Zeta Reticuli
A thrilling action-packed Sci-fi deep space adventure.
A Novel By Gerry A. Saunders

A sample from my next book, Book 1

Battles at Zeta Reticuli.

The Eyes of Devastation.

Suddenly, the view screens flared white, then went blank as Andromeda plunged straight into the force field protecting 'Axon's' ship.

Axon was the Commander of one of the best battlecruisers in the Crillon Empire. He had been ordered to stay behind for two days. And was about to leave to catch up with the main fleet already heading to Sector 2.

Searing heat and giddiness came like ripples on a pond as Andromeda struggled to fight the entangled force fields. A thin line of crackling raw energy began to separate the two ships.

And Andromeda's tactical screen came back online as they came closer to separation. Then a solution surged into Andromeda's and Frank's minds.

"Don't separate us," Frank yelled, even though he knew that Andromeda could read his tactical thoughts.

"He won't be able to jump!"

With its force field flaring and shimmering, the Crillon ship faced a massive planet no more than sixty kilometers away and seemingly full of devastation.

Andromeda now began to push against the alien's force field. Neither could fire weapons while both ships' force fields were interlinked without destroying each other.

Slowly but inevitably, the two ships drifted toward the planet's surface, now only forty kilometers below them. Their force fields sparkled like a firework display feeding on thin air.

"Captain," Ned Parker called, sounding panicky. "There's an energy build-up starting at the back end of the alien ship."

"We see it, Ned. Can we disrupt it?"

"No. Neither of us can fire."

"OK, so why would the alien ship waste power that he can't use? Keep an eye on it, Ned, while we search for a solution."

"Will do," and he was gone.

"What's the alien ship doing?" Alan asked.

"He's trying to turn towards us to take a shot," Andromeda replied. "But, each time he tries, I can still stop him."

The view of the planet's devastation now showed on the screen. Together with the alien ship bobbing around, trying to break free from Andromeda.

"Eighteen kilometers," Andromeda warned. "We'll soon have to break free. The planet's atmosphere is strengthening, and it's starting to affect my screens."

The side of the alien's force field closest to the planet took the brunt of its atmospherical effects. And was steadily shrinking with every second that passed.

The alien's ship was now just seven kilometers from the surface and being pushed harder and harder. Until suddenly, its force field's integrity failed. Then the copper-colored outer coating of the alien's ship peeled off in a violent swarm of deadly metal panels, leaving the skeletal body plunging towards the planet.

Andromeda struggled to overcome the gravitational pull and destruction just seconds away from her.

Frank wanted to yell, "Brace for impact."

But didn't.

End of sample

About the Author

I started writing my first science-fiction novel some years ago. But fate then conspired to point me in a different direction. Even though my electronic design career was exciting and fulfilling, especially with the technology's fast-moving pace. I never lost my love of Space or the possibility of man traveling in Space and colonizing planets one day.

It wasn't until 2013 that I had time to continue writing my first book, Battles at Zeta Reticuli.

Set in the Twenty-Fourth Century, with a storyline based on the StarShip Andromeda and her crew. In book one, Andromeda's advanced self-aware AI was on a rapid learning curve.

Andromeda had been designed to interact with her Captain and crew. Unlike the mechanical-sounding AIs in many Sci-fi stories. Instead, she would sound human and alive. While her crew's transceiver implant links with Andromeda almost made her a living entity. And enabled her to perform virtually all operational needs while providing an organic feel to the ship.

Gerry A. Saunders

Dedication

I'd like to thank my wife for her support in helping me complete this book. I hope you enjoyed this as much as I have enjoyed writing it.

Other Books by this Author

SpaceFed StarShips Trilogy.

Book 1.   Battles at Zeta Reticuli.

Book 2.   Battle for Delta Pavonis.

Book 3.   An Alliance at Kepler.

SpaceFed StarShips Series.

Book 4.   Death of Time.

Book 5.   Acarea. A Triumph or Disaster.

Book 6.   The Garoden War. Part 1. Into the Fire.

Book 7.   The Garoden War. Part 2. Military Gamble.

Book 8.   Galactic War. (Up Time, Down).

Book 9.   Battle for Time.

Plus: The Definitive StarShips Trilogy, in one book.

   The Martian Factor   (Prequel)

   http://www.spacefedbooks.com

Printed in Great Britain
by Amazon